Love in Oxley Crossing

Book 1

Australian Rural Romance

Marrying Alan Morgan

LENA WEST

Gymea Publishing

Published by Gymea Publishing

https://www.facebook.com/LenaWestAuthor/

www.lenawestauthor.com

ISBN-13: 978-0-6482110-0-6

Disclaimer

This story is a work of fiction.

Names, characters, places and incidents are the product of the author's imagination and are used fictitiously. Any resemblance to events, locales or actual persons, living or dead, is entirely coincidental.

Some actual locations may be referenced in passing.

Table of Contents

MARRYING ALAN MORGAN

Dedication

To Glenda – without whom my writing career would never have begun, with thanks for her encouragement and untiring support.

MARRYING ALAN MORGAN

1

Oxley Crossing. Alan

The sun was low on the horizon as Alan Morgan parked the quad in the open sided machinery shed. Two kelpies leapt from their perch behind him frolicking around his legs when he dismounted. Dust clung to the sweat-stained work-shirt sticking uncomfortably to his broad, well-muscled torso, making him think longingly of a shower, closely followed by a cold beer.

Soon, he promised himself. Briefly raising the battered, black Akubra, he swiped a tanned forearm over wet, springy dark curls which could do with a trim.

"Well done, you two," he praised the dogs, stooping to pat them affectionately. "You've put in a good day's work, haven't you?"

He continued his words of praise and thanks as he refuelled the quad ready for the morning. Cass and Baron had put in as long, hot and dusty a day as himself, moving sheep from bare, brown hillsides down onto the creek flats where there was still abundant natural fodder. They were top dogs, bred here on 'Morgan's Run' by his father, Andrew; a nationally acclaimed expert when it came to the breeding, training and showing of quality sheep dogs. The kennels supplemented the property's income very nicely, since no farmer could afford to pay men to do work dogs had proved themselves capable of. Not even farmers as comfortably off as the Morgans; although it hadn't always been so.

Over a hundred years earlier, Tobias Morgan and his sons, William and Patrick, had followed in the wake of the government surveyor, John Oxley; being the first to take up land on the rich alluvial flats bordering the creek he named for his own family, near what was now Oxley Crossing. From humble beginnings, the Morgans had prospered, surviving droughts, floods, bushfires and wars. While never numbered among the squattocracy, the pastoral elite, they were comfortably established pillars of local society. People looked up to the Morgans. Trusted them. And Alan had never doubted his place as the next Morgan of 'Morgan's Run'.

All of this was far from his mind, though, as he whistled the dogs to heel, returning them to the kennels and checking their food and water bowls. *You never hear them moaning and complaining,* Alan reminded himself, as with a final pat and word of praise for a job well done, he turned towards his own quarters. The dogs loved to work. Thrived on it; rewarding a humane master with unswerving loyalty. *Unlike humans.*

Alan's morose thoughts dwelt on the woman whose bitter complaints were making his life such a misery of late. He often found himself stringing his jobs out to avoid spending time in the house with her. The previous month had been a blessed respite, with Janice visiting her family in Sydney.

A mixed blessing though.

He missed the kids. Missed their innocent prattle and insatiable curiosity. Missed the warmth of their ready hugs and kisses. A son would be pretty good, he sometimes thought, but he wouldn't swap his two little girls for a dozen sons. Melanie and Jocelyn were the joy of his life. So far, the tension between Janice and himself didn't appear to have affected them, and if he had any say in the matter, it wouldn't.

They were due home today, he remembered, quickening his steps. Unless Janice had changed her mind. Again. She had deferred her return once already. Alan strained his ears as he jogged towards his house and the shower he badly needed after trailing behind a mob of sheep all day.

The distant sound of high-pitched squeals of glee from the direction of the main house, mingling with the bass rumblings of his father's voice and the thuds of a football being kicked back and forth, lifted his heart.

Relieved, he grinned, picturing the game in progress. If he was honest with himself, he wouldn't have been surprised if Janice had decided not to return at all. It had been in her mind, he was sure, following that last row before her departure. Except for the danger of losing his girls, he wouldn't have cared; almost bringing their differences into the open then and there.

A man not given to introspection, he had spent a lot of hours during this last month examining the state of his marriage; finally deciding to talk it out with Jan and see if they couldn't do better. It wasn't good for the girls, seeing them fighting and arguing over every little thing.

Theirs had not been a union made in Heaven; however, they had both started out determined to make a success story of it, shaky beginning or not. They had so much going for them, it was difficult for him to understand why their marriage was coming apart at the seams. He was certain they could rediscover that initial optimism and turn their marriage around. If they pulled together, and placed the girls first.

Unfortunately, Janice, the pampered only child of the wealthy property developer, Robert Baldry, her name on every hostess's A-list, had never taken to life as a farmer's wife. Or as a mother. Though he believed she did genuinely love Melanie and Jocelyn, he also knew she often saw them as something of a millstone holding her back. Her intention had been to follow in her father's footsteps, learning his family business from the ground up, and one day succeeding him. During recent months, she had been suggesting he leave the farm and head back to Sydney with her. He shook his head and sighed. He was a farmer, what would he do in the Big Smoke?

~~~~~

About to head in the direction of the ballgame, he decided to go home first and clean up. Then he'd be free to relax with his family.

He was glad they were at his parent's place; it would be easier meeting Janice in company. He was in no hurry to rush into what he knew was going to be a difficult conversation.

It wasn't until he was pulling on fresh jeans and neatly pressed khaki shirt that another possibility occurred to him. Unpalatable, but easier for him to understand. Was there another man? One who could give Janice all she wanted?

~~~~~

Melanie broke off her attack on the ball at the first squeak of the garden gate. Glancing up expectantly, her face became one huge grin, and she took off at top speed to be whirled up in a strong pair of arms.

"Daddy! Daddy! We're home at last!" shrieked the tawny-blonde tomboy.

"Me too, Daddy! Me Too!" Three-year old Jocelyn, half the age of her older sister, her body still retaining the chubbiness of infancy, tugged on her father's jeans. Swinging Melanie onto one hip, Alan bent to scoop up his precious baby.

"You too, Darling," he agreed.

Burying his face in Jocelyn's dark curls to hide the moisture gathering in his eyes, he breathed in his favourite perfume – the innocent blend of baby shampoo and perspiration of a healthy, outdoors child. "Umm," he hugged them both tightly to his chest. "Melanie. Jocelyn. I've really missed my girls. You've been gone such a long time."

"We missed you too, Daddy," Melanie assured him. Her sweet kiss on his left cheek was promptly matched by a wet, sloppy kiss from Jocelyn on the other cheek. "We had lots of fun with Gran and Grandpa and Uncle Julian and Mummy, but it would have been ever so much better with you, too."

Uncle Julian? A hot, jealous flame burned in Alan's heart. This was the first he'd heard of any Uncle Julian, and he made a mental note to follow it up. Later.

Suppressing a sigh, he let the children slip down his body, steadying them till they found their feet, and allowed his eyes to come to rest on the petite, smartly-dressed blonde leaning tensely against the veranda rail.

Taking a small hand in each of his much larger ones, he pinned a carefully welcoming smile on his wide, sensuous lips and set off across the lawn.

"Welcome home, Janice", he called as soon as they came within speaking range, noting wryly that both his parents had discreetly absented themselves, granting them privacy for their reunion. Mounting the three shallow steps onto the veranda, he released the girls' hands, reaching out to embrace his wife.

"Alan," was all she said, her voice cool as she stepped unhurriedly out of the embrace which, her husband noted cynically, hadn't been returned. "How have you been?"

"Lonely," was his instant reply. "I've missed you, Jan."

"Really?" she murmured. "I was under the impression my absence might be preferable to my presence."

Alan groaned silently. *Looks like she's planning on taking up right where we left off.*

Aloud, he said, "We need to talk, Jan, but can't we leave it till later?" he gestured towards the children who had run to meet his parents, returning to the garden laden with drinks and a tray of appetisers.

"Hello, Dear," his mother greeted him warmly. "I thought we could all have dinner together, since Janice has been driving most of the day. We'll have it early, then you can take these two imps home to bed."

"It seemed a sensible idea, Alan," Janice shrugged. "Especially since I have no idea what's available at our place."

Alan nodded his agreement, all too aware of his almost empty fridge. During the past month he'd eaten with his parents more often than he had at his own house. Gratefully, he accepted the cold beer his father thrust into his hand.

The conversation naturally centred around the trip to Sydney, and Uncle Julian's named was innocently mentioned several more times by the girls. However, when Alan raised an enquiring eyebrow towards his wife, she turned away from him; lips tight, not deigning to throw light on either the man's presence or his identity.

Alan let it go. For the time being.

$$\sim\sim\sim\sim\sim$$

"Go on with you," Barbara, Alan's mother, laughed, shooing her guests on their way. "There's only a few things to pop in the dishwasher, and I can handle that without extra help. You two must be dying to be alone, so off you go."

A flurry of hugs and goodnight kisses, and the younger Morgans, their children swinging from their hands between them, set off across the crest of the hill to the second house, nestled into a hollow half-way down the other side. It had originally been built to accommodate a married farmhand, long since retired, and when Alan had returned from University with a pregnant wife, Andrew and Barbara had had it refurbished for them; deeming it unlikely a modern bride would want to share a house with her in-laws.

∾∾∾∾∾

"You said earlier that we need to talk. I agree. We do." Janice was standing in the centre of the lounge room, and now that Alan had joined her after reading the girls their bedtime story and tucking them in for the night, she led the way out to the kitchen, closing the door behind them in the hope their voices wouldn't disturb the children.

"That's right. We've let our marriage deteriorate, which is every bit my fault as much as yours. I think we need to sort out our differences ASAP, and come up with a way to get this marriage back on track." They had gravitated to chairs across the kitchen table from each other, and as he finished speaking, Alan reached out, taking both of Janice's hands in his.

For a moment, she let him, then gently withdrew them. Determination in every inch of her rigidly straight back, she met him eye to eye. "That's just it, Alan," Janice exclaimed, voice chillingly firm. "I don't believe we can. We've tried before, and it didn't work then. Not for any length of time. Did it?"

8

She was referring to the time several years earlier when they had thought another baby would heal the growing rift between them. For a while, their excitement and joy in Jocelyn's advent had drawn them together. Unfortunately, the respite had been short-lived.

Stubborn to the core, Alan clamped his lips together.

"We tried our best, Alan." Janice was determined to persuade him to her view. "But, you know the problems go too deep for easy solutions. It's me, really, I suppose. You're a good man, Alan. A terrific father; and with the right woman I believe you'd be a great husband, too. Only I'm not the right woman. We simply don't love each other; and never did." She could see an all too familiar anger surging up inside Alan, and sought to forestall its eruption. "Think, Alan," she leaned across the table, laying an urgent hand upon his. "If it hadn't been for Melanie, we would have gone our separate ways when you left uni. We had a lot of fun together, and we liked each other a lot, but we were never in love, were we?"

Janice's ruthless honesty gave Alan pause. He pushed his chair back, moving to stand at the window. Hands thrust deep in his pockets, he stared into the darkness. He grunted assent, and, relieved, Janice continued.

"I thought love would grow." she whispered, sad it hadn't. "As you did, also, I think. Maybe if I'd been a different type of woman, it might have. Only, I'm still a city girl at heart, Alan," she explained. "I've tried to take an interest in the country scene, only it just doesn't do it for me. I feel stifled. Trapped; with only the house and the kids. I love our girls, but being a mum isn't enough for me."

"Well, what more do you want?" Pent-up frustration made Alan's tone more aggressive than he'd intended, and Janice shrank away from him. Breathing deeply, he controlled his anger; and yes, he admitted, his fear. Deep down, he recognised his anger as a cover-up to hide the fear curling icy tendrils around his heart. Making a discernible effort to speak more moderately, he asked again. "What *do* you want, Jan? Tell me."

"I want my old life back. I want my career back. I want to live where there are people with more conversation than bloody sheep. People who share my interest in music and theatre and art. Oh, and so very much more. I want to have those things as an integral part of my daily life; not just when I go home on a visit."

She pleaded with her eyes for him to understand.

Alan felt helpless pain, recognising that Janice didn't think of 'Morgan's Run' as home; and probably never had.

"It sounds selfish, I know, but I feel I'm withering inside. Dying mentally." Her words choked off on a half sob, and she covered her face with hands that trembled uncontrollably.

Alan stared at her, helpless to offer comfort. This was what he'd feared lay at the core of his wife's discontent. He had no idea how to counter it.

"My life is here, Jan," he said, voice low and heavy with regret. "I'd give you everything you want, if I could. What would I do in the city, though? You say you're dying here in the country, but I'd feel exactly like that in the city. I enjoyed myself at uni, but at the back of my mind I always knew it was temporary, and I'd be coming home when I finished."

Thoroughly miserable, Janice acknowledged the truth of his statement. "I know." She hated hurting this man who had been her husband for close on seven years. She studied him through a blur of tears. Tall and lean, with the blue eyes and black hair of his Welsh forebears, his weather-toughened face was craggily handsome. Throw in 'Morgan's Run', and he was quite a catch.

Only not for me, she sorrowed. *If he wasn't such a good man, kind and gentle with those he loved, intelligent and skilled in his work, a true man of the land, this would all have been so much easier.* She pulled her thoughts up at that point. There was no future for her with Alan Morgan. During her month away, she had argued it all out with herself, over and over, and felt certain she was doing the only thing which would ensure a chance of happiness; for the both of them. It was not a decision entered into lightly.

Firm and sure, she quelled her tears. "I want a divorce, Alan. I only came back here to talk to you in person, and pack my things. Then I'm leaving." There, she'd said it. It was real now. Janice held herself apart as Alan, white and tense, sank back onto his chair.

"Just like that?" he protested. "No discussion? No trying to compromise?"

"No. It's not 'just like that'. I've worn myself out thinking about it. Trying to find a different solution. There isn't one. This isn't easy for me, you know." She jumped up and paced to the end of the room, whirling about to face him. "It's the last resort," she stated, pugnacious and determined.

Alan was standing too, now, facing her; his breathing rapid, fists clenched, and a flush of temper had replaced the stricken pallor.

"And I suppose 'Uncle Julian' had nothing to do with your decision? All this talk about being stifled to death is a cover-up for the fact you've found someone else, isn't it?"

"That's not fair, Alan," Janice retorted. "I've told you the truth. Julian Conway had nothing to do with it."

"You expect me to believe that?" Alan sneered.

"You'll believe what you like, no matter what I say, so I won't bother to defend myself."

"Because you know your actions are indefensible!"

Both their voices were raised now, their reasonable, logical discussion degenerating into a slanging match. With a visible effort, Janice turned away, to stare out into the night, regathering her thoughts. She wasn't leaving Alan for Julian, who was gay; however, meeting him had played a part in crystallising her ambitions.

One day, though, there might be another man who would be important to her. How to explain to Alan? She knew she couldn't and decided to let it go.

Alan waited, white-knuckled hands gripping the back of a chair.

"I'm leaving you, Alan," Janice repeated. "Tomorrow. I don't need your permission, or anything else. Dad's given me back my old job and I've signed a lease on a flat."

She kept her back to her husband, watching him in the window reflection. It seemed forever before he spoke.

"I see," he uttered, cold as an Antarctic blast.

"You never intended to even consider repairing our marriage, did you? Only tearing it apart. Well, you can have your divorce, Jan. Go tomorrow if that's what you want, and don't come back. But don't you even think of taking Melanie and Jocelyn with you. They're my daughters and they'll be staying right here. With me." His mouth snapped shut and he stared implacably at his wife's back, unmoved when her shoulders shook with her sobs.

"They're my daughters too, Alan," she wept. "I love them too. Think of all the things they're missing out on here," she pleaded. "There's so much I could give them if they lived in Sydney."

"What about the things I can give them? You know how they love the farm, and the animals and everything. They're country kids, Jan. They don't belong in the city. They stay here. With me." Adamant, he reiterated his stand.

This, too, Janice had foreseen; and already come to terms with. This was the price of her freedom. She had known from the first, Alan would never let his girls go without a fight. Her protest had been a forlorn hope, now set aside, although not without bitter regret.

"Can we reach a compromise, Alan? I'd like to avoid one of those horribly destructive tug-of-love cases?" Sadly, she brushed her tears aside. "If I let them stay with you, will you allow them to be with me during school holidays? Please, Alan, don't shut me out of their lives entirely."

Stunned, Alan stared at Janice in disbelief. He knew she loved the girls as much as he did.

That she was willing to make such a heart-rending sacrifice, was testimony to how seriously she wanted a divorce.

"We'll work out a civilised arrangement," he promised, turning away from the sight of her tear-streaked face.

He said the words, but bitterness against city women to whom career was more important than children and family hardened his heart.

He would keep his girls safe; and he would never be taken in again.

2

Sydney, 2 years later. Angie.

"Damn it all, Angie, I've got to let you go. You can see the bind I'm in here, can't you? The man is too influential for me to offend him by keeping you on. You're out, girl. No more arguments." Red faced and spluttering with annoyance, the huge man seemed about to pop a gasket. Not that Angie Wilson cared tuppence if he did, the fat toad. Arms akimbo, the feisty redhead glared defiance at the loose-jowled face looming over her, invading her space.

"Instead of sacking me, you ought to be defending me!" she hissed. "That rotten creep treats me as if barmaid is a euphemism for 'whore'. I'm telling you, Max, his behaviour is intolerable. He deserved what he got; and more." Angie stamped her foot in righteous fury.

"And you're a trouble-maker, Angie Wilson. From your first day on the job, you've been wasting my time complaining and bitching over nothing," the belligerent, grossly obese man interrupted. "You're lucky you've lasted this long."

"Nothing!" Angie screeched, her normally smiling green eyes reduced to narrow slits spitting venomous sparks. Her previous differences with her boss flashed across her mind, chief amongst them her objections to the uniform he insisted the female bar staff wear – an almost non-existent, red micro-mini teemed with an embarrassingly low cut, see-through, black blouse.

She couldn't stand the way Max Porterman's sleazy clientele leered down the front of her blouse and waited for her to lean over the tables, trying to look under her skirt. She had absolutely no doubt this overly provocative uniform was the cause of most of the problems she'd been having with certain of the customers in this supposedly exclusive private club.

She was reminded all over again of tonight's grievance Sure, her instinctive reaction had put her in the wrong, but she had no intention of admitting it to this fat slob.

"You call it nothing," she reiterated, returning to the fray. "That dirty animal is forever mauling me and making lewd suggestions; and you call it nothing!"

"Mauling!" Her boss snorted. "A little pat on the fanny occasionally."

"If a pat on the fanny was all it was, I could have ignored it," she snapped back, "only tonight he went further than that." She snorted her disgust.

"The filthy swine shoved his hand up under this pathetic excuse for a skirt you insist I wear, and groped me while I was serving his table. Don't you dare call it nothing, Max Porterman!" Becoming aware her voice was rising to a near scream, she drew a deep breath and consciously moderated her tone.

"I call it sexual assault," she hissed. "If I could afford a decent lawyer I'd have him up on a charge."

"Well, you blew any chance of that when you upended that tray of drinks into his lap. And you blew your job, too. Get your things and get out of here."

A tiny glow of rebellious satisfaction warmed Angie as she recalled the incident, her mouth twitching into a tight-lipped grimace half way to a smile.

Maybe it had cost her this miserable job, but it had been worth it; although she'd miss the fatter than usual pay-checks, which had been its sole drawcard. That creep's loss of face in front of his cronies had made up for quite a few of the insults he'd heaped on her since she began working here. As for the job, it was no loss.

Coming to work here had been a huge mistake all round, regardless of the higher pay. Now things had come to a head, Angie couldn't wait to be shot of the crummy joint with its lousy boss and even lousier clientele. Her temper was cooling now, though, into an icy determination.

I had better start taking care of myself, she decided.

It was a sure thing no-one else would.

"Come on, Max," she cajoled in a near normal tone. "Admit.it. I was totally justified in retaliating."

Max's piggy eyes, almost lost in the folds of fat surrounding them, assumed a surly, calculating glint. *I've got the red-haired bitch now,* he exulted. *In a minute, she'll be begging me to take her back.* Gloating, the bully savoured a vision of making Angie crawl. Then, when her abasement was complete, he'd boot her out on her sexy little backside into the gutter.

He'd seriously misjudged matters when he hired her, thinking her opulent charms would be to his advantage. Instead, her unexpected prudery made her a liability instead. *Well, that little mistake is about to be rectified.* He licked his lips in anticipation.

Max Porterman had miscalculated, thinking he had the street-wise Angie Wilson at his mercy. She'd witnessed the bullying publican in action before; throwing his not inconsiderable weight around amongst the more defenceless members of his staff.

Forewarned, she'd taken the precaution of arming herself against the inevitable day when it would be her turn on the receiving end of his bombast. Now looked like an appropriate time to teach him she wouldn't be intimidated. Not by the likes of him.

"I want out of here even more than you want me gone," she stated calmly. "I'll go, all right, just as soon as you pay me the wages I'm owed, plus a week's severance pay in lieu of notice. Oh, and you'd better write me a reference, too. A good one."

References were important when you had a living to earn, and Angie reckoned she'd earned one of the best during her time in this dump. She stared adamantly into Porterman's dumbstruck countenance, plonking herself down in the straight-backed wooden chair in front of his desk, crossing her legs and leaning back more confidently than she actually felt.

"I'm not leaving empty-handed, Max," she informed him straitly. It was a favourite trick of Porterman's, throwing people out without paying them the money they were owed, and his chagrined expression confirmed the accuracy of her assumption. *The fat pig intended to gyp me too, and it just isn't on*. Before Porterman could get back in stride, Angie played her ace.

"If I don't get my money and my reference, I'll be having a word with the cops about the goings-on in your back room, Max. I've got plenty of proof," she informed him in a silky voice, "and don't think I won't use it. I will."

A short while later, Angie Wilson, reference and money stowed securely in her handbag, shook off the dust of Porterman's club and climbed into the back seat of the taxi she had felt it prudent to call. She had made enemies tonight, she knew, so it wouldn't be a wise idea to look for a new job anywhere in this vicinity. Which reminded her of the next problem looming on her horizon.

What with Sydney's exorbitant rents, food and public transport; being out of work was going to deplete her savings too rapidly for comfort.

A new position was an urgent priority.

When she shared her news with them, her two flatmates had plenty of moral support, but no practical suggestions to offer, so Angie retired to her room to do some serious thinking. For some time now, she had been feeling increasingly dissatisfied.

City living had long since lost whatever gloss it had once had, and although she had numerous acquaintances, Angie was appalled to realise how very, very few true friends she had.

No-one would miss me if I were to up and leave town tomorrow, she mused, a despondent droop to her perfect cupid's bow lips. Then she sat up with a jerk, and ran the thought by herself again.

Leave Sydney?

Could she? Should she?

The longer she considered it, the more right it felt. No-one else would be disadvantaged, certainly not her flatmates who would quickly replace her the same way they'd found her; through an ad online, after she'd walked out on that weasel, Luke Freemont, her two-timing boyfriend. *Men are the pits,* she thought, disgusted. *At least the ones who come my way are.*

Once she had been a romantic innocent, dreaming dreams of idyllic love and happy ever after. Now and then she still caught her mind drifting nostalgically among the clouds, even though life had taught her otherwise.

Love existed. But romantic love was a myth. The stuff of little girls' dreams.

Life was what you made it.

And isn't that the truth, she told herself, bringing her mind to bear once again on her present dilemma. *I'll do it!* She decided. *I'll leave Sydney. Not much I can do about it tonight, though.*

She turned out the lights and snuggled beneath the blankets, still turning over alternatives in her mind.

~~~~~

Angie had grown up in country Victoria, running away from home to seek her fortune in the city when she was only fifteen. *Except it wasn't the country I was running from*, she reminded herself.

Actually, she discovered she had a great many fond memories of the small town where she'd lived as a child.

The real problem had been her step-father. A man way too free with his hands, in more ways than one. Neither had there been much love coming her way from her mother, a woman wholly bound up in herself and pitifully denying her years.

Once the acknowledged local belle, her teenaged daughter, with her curvaceous figure, vibrant red curls and sparkling green eyes, posed a threat to the woman's self-image.

Without her mother's support, the young Angie Wilson had found life in her stepfather's house insupportable.

On arrival in Sydney, she had stayed in a women's hostel for a time while she worked double shifts in a fast-food restaurant to pay her way. At eighteen, and fully independent, she had fallen in love for the first time with Cory Ireland, and moved in with him. He had been instrumental in helping her to find better paying work behind the bar in his favourite pub.

By the time the affair fizzled out, she had grown to like bar work. She enjoyed working amongst people, liked most of the customers, and was stimulated by the saucy banter which formed an integral part of the job. Cheerful, quick and efficient, she was popular with customers and bosses alike.

Porterman had been the exception.

Vaguely ashamed of her aborted education, she had taken TAFE classes, emerging with satisfying grades and her Higher School Certificate. Originally planning to go further with her studies, she had fallen under Luke Freemont's spell, and her ambitions abruptly took a back seat.

Luke had had grandiose ideas about going into business for himself; and, with nebulous hints of marriage sometime in the glorious future, had persuaded Angie to invest her hard-earned savings in his venture.

Needing stitches when she cut her hand on a broken glass, she had returned home early one evening, to find Luke entertaining another girl. In bed. That was the end as far as Angie was concerned.

Injury was added to insult when she attempted to reclaim her money. Luke's business morals being as delinquent as his personal ones, her money was long gone.

Bitterly chastened, she had cut her losses, put man and lost savings down to experience, and begun anew. Now she had it all to do again.

Angie thumped her pillow. Sloughing off her painful recollections, she rolled over, seeking sleep. Essentially an optimist, she chose to look on the bright side. It had been her intention to part company with Porterman soon anyway. A current tightening of the job market had been all that was holding her back.

Getting sacked, she comforted herself, *isn't the end. It's a gateway opening onto countless new opportunities.*

Morning saw Angie wake, her resolve to exit Sydney with all speed even stronger. Hard-won caution played Devil's Advocate, though. Alone after the other girls left for work, she sat down with a mug of coffee to consider her plan in detail.

Last night, smarting from the ignominy of being sacked, she had been flying high on a cocktail of adrenalin and emotion. In the bright light of day, she tried for a more pragmatic approach.

In Sydney's teeming millions, Angie Wilson was no more than a faceless, voiceless statistic. What if she burnt her bridges, heading west of the Divide, only to discover too late she was even more dissatisfied? But in Sydney she had no sense of place or belonging. Nobody greeted her by name and stopped to chat when she walked down the street. Unlike the small town she grew up in.

And, she reminded herself, *if I'm not happy, I can always move on.* Yes. She would take the plunge; but sensibly.

Carefully she compiled a list of what she considered the absolute minimum of basic requirements for a comfortable life. Working conditions aside, most of the items on her list were related to ways to fill her daylight hours.

Evenings being her normal work hours, she had become largely dependent on her local gym, with reading and craft activities taking up the slack. And study, of course. Away from Luke's poisonous influence, she had resumed her studies, signing up for a two-year TAFE online Hospitality course which would qualify her for a job in resort or event management. Junior management, but a huge step forward, out of the bar.

Being online, she could continue her studies anywhere. With hard work, and diligent saving, maybe one day she would even be able to realise her most cherished dream; that of having her own B&B in some tourist hotspot where she'd be able to attract enough guests to make a decent living.

Back to the list.

Would a small place have a gym? Maybe not. She crossed out gym and replaced it with 'swimming pool' and 'exercise classes'. *It's the country, so there should be some nice walks as well. I'll be sure to ask. And if there are no exercise classes, I can start my own.*

A tingle of excitement started in her belly. She had never seen herself as a leader, but perhaps she should broaden her horizons. At this moment, she felt anything was possible. 'Find a congenial group of women to join.' was added to her list. In this optimistic mood, she was prepared to view potential drawbacks as challenges and opportunities.

My life is what I make it, she told herself, *and I'm more than ready to look at new options.*

Over the next few days, Angie patiently scanned the vacancies until she found one which resonated with her. An experienced person was needed in the progressive community (the ad claimed) of Oxley Crossing, west of Tamworth (which she knew to be a sizable rural city). At 'The Victoria Inn', an historic coaching inn built in 1872. Accommodation provided; so that essential requirement was taken care of.

She wondered exactly what 'progressive community' meant? It sounded promising. The whole tone of the ad had a pleasant feel to it. A quick browse through Google provided more information. The local council website contained an impressive list of organisations and sporting clubs.

No gym, she noted, *but they do have an Olympic sized swimming pool. Tennis,* she read on. *It might be fun to give it a try.* There didn't seem to be many shops, but there was a regular bus into Tamworth. *Anyway*, she comforted her inner shopaholic, *no shops, means I'll be able to save and get ahead.*

Crossing her fingers for luck, she rang the number given in the ad. Applicants were advised to apply in writing, but it couldn't hurt to show a bit of enthusiasm.

"The Victoria. Phil Morris speaking," drawled a pleasant baritone. "You're speaking to him," it continued when Angie asked for the manager. "My wife and I are owner-operators. How may I help you?"

Phil Morris sounded decent. Angie introduced herself and stated her business. After Max Porterman, a married couple had a reassuring ring.

They chatted a few minutes longer, Phil patiently answering her questions about both the advertised job, and the town itself.

"Mr Morris," Angie said, cautiously enthusiastic, "both 'The Victoria' and Oxley Crossing sound just what I'm looking for." A warm chuckle greeted her statement.

"In that case, Ms Wilson, I'll hand you over to my wife. Marge will sort out your application. If the three of us are satisfied with each other, maybe I'll be seeing you soon."

Marge Morris sounded as warm and friendly as her husband, further reassuring Angie. "You are keen, Ms Wilson," she said. "I like that. Now, let's get down to practicalities. Why don't you email me your resume, then after Phil and I have considered it, I'll be in touch."

Angie quickly agreed, and, resume already prepared, sent it off immediately. On the strength of her warm reception from the Morris's, she went out to her favourite coffee shop and splurged on lunch. A sale sign in the dress shop next door tempted her in. She found two stylish skirts which showed off her long legs to advantage without sacrificing one iota of dignity.

She had mentioned Porterman's uniforms to Marge Morris, who had answered tartly, "There'll be nothing of that kind here, Ms Wilson. My girls are encouraged to look nice without being scandalous."

Angie could have cheered.

Angie leaned back against the headrest, closing her eyes as the bus driver moved up through the gears. Taking a deep breath, she opened them again to watch Sydney's familiar suburbs disappear one by one behind her, until they turned onto the freeway.

Less than a week had elapsed since she'd first spoken to the Morris's. Marge had called her back the same evening, offering her the position, which she had promptly accepted. Her room in the flat had been snapped up by a friend of one of the other girls, who had even been willing to buy Angie's furniture and other bits and pieces she couldn't take with her.

Except for an overnight case, the rest of her things had been freighted directly to 'The Victoria' where she trusted they were now awaiting her arrival. Settling down for the long journey, she opened the new bestseller by her favourite author.

~~~~~

Tucking her book into the side pocket of her handbag, Angie began eagerly observing the country they were passing through. She had changed buses in Tamworth, and now, according to the signpost she'd glimpsed a moment ago, they were only fifteen kilometres from her destination. Oxley Crossing. A tiny shiver ran up her spine.

The broad paddocks on either side of the road were dotted with sheep and cattle; the pastures being interspersed with acres and acres of grain crops stretching to the horizon.

She observed farm houses, several of which appeared to be gracious old homesteads, nestled within sheltering groves of trees; islands of green scattered across a sea of rolling brown and gold hills. 'Emmmaroo'; 'Branson Park'; 'Yeldaran'; 'Morgan's Run'; 'Upson Downs'; Angie grinned at that one, enchanted by the poetry of the names she read on mailboxes and gates.Oxley Crossing straddled Morgan's Creek, she recalled from the town's website, wondering if there was a connection with the property they had just passed.

They rumbled across the bridge shortly, 'The Victoria Inn' coming into sight with a row of shops straggling up the street beyond. A park and cricket ground were opposite. Footpath plantings of flowering trees and annuals made an attractive show.

A smile lit up Angie's expressive face signalling her delight with her first view of her new home.

"Here you are, Luv," the bus driver cheerily called over his shoulder. "The old 'Vic'. A grand old pub in its heyday, and picking up again under the new owners, from what I hear."

The bus groaned to a halt outside the main entrance. Angie picked up her things and stepped down slowly, eyes busily drinking in the elegance of the red brick and iron lace façade of the two-story hotel.

It wasn't the official stop. However, there being nobody else waiting, the amiable driver hadn't seen the point of making her walk from the service station when he went right past where she was going. Angie appreciated the small courtesy, which seemed to confirm her hopes of what to expect from country folks.

3

Hanging up the last of her clothes in the roomy, old-fashioned wardrobe, Angie nested her smaller cases inside the larger, and hoisted them on top of the wardrobe where they were effectively hidden by a decorative panel above its doors. Glancing at her watch, she saw there was time for a quick shower and change of clothes before dinner. She smiled, recalling Marge's effusive welcome.

"Oh," she had exclaimed," aren't you the pretty one Ms Wilson."

"Angie please, Mrs Morris." Rosy cheeked, Angie had been warmed by the older woman' spontaneous compliment.

"Of course, Dear. I'd like that. And we're Marge and Phil. We're all one big happy family here at the old 'Vic', aren't we Phil?"

Marge, her Thatcher-style blonde helmet rigidly immaculate, turned for corroboration to her burly, silver-haired husband; a man of medium height who appeared to be about a decade older than his plump, talkative wife.

"Sure are," he said, a twinkle in his eye. "Welcome, Angie. I put your stuff in your room when it arrived, so if you're okay with that little bag, I'll be off to check the stock." He cast an appreciative glance over the new barmaid's attractive assets, adding with a grin, "Could be a full house come Friday."

"Now that's enough of that, Phil," his wife reprimanded him. "You'll be giving Angie a poor opinion of us." She turned anxiously towards Angie, earnestly assuring her, "We don't exploit our girls like your last boss, Angie, but there's no denying a pretty girl behind the bar does bring the boys flocking in from miles around."

"It's all right, Marge," Angie assured her. "I'm quite realistic. There's an enormous difference between being appreciated and being used, isn't there?"

Phil had disappeared, leaving Marge to show Angie around after they'd shared a welcoming cup of tea. 'The Victoria' wasn't particularly big; its limited accommodations had been supplemented by a gleaming, freshly built row of motel units and a small caravan park out the back.

"This town is ideally situated for a weekend getaway," Marge had explained. "We're starting to get quite a few people coming up from the coast to see what the inland areas have to offer. When you look around, you'll see we have plenty to attract visitors."

Marge, an enthusiastic promoter of her town. continued. "Phil and I saw the potential, and made sure we were ready. We've been lobbying council and state tourist authorities, and at last we've got ourselves on the map."

Beginning to understand what was meant by the reference to a 'progressive community', Angie was impressed. Oxley Crossing was a town on the move, with the Morris's leading the way. The tour over, Marge had shown her to this comfortable room overlooking the old stables, now used as garages and general storage. Her cases and boxes were stacked neatly against the wall. Making a mental note to thank Phil, she had busied herself with her unpacking.

"You don't have to live in," Marge had assured her, "only there isn't really anywhere else, unless you want to rent a house. Our other staff are all married women who have their own homes and families. You'll have the women's bathroom at this end of the corridor to yourself except when we're full up."

"I've never lived in before," Angie said, "but you've made me so comfortable, I doubt I'll be in a hurry to look elsewhere."

∿∿∿∿∿

I definitely won't be in a hurry to move out, Angie thought later, contentedly draining the teapot dry. *If this was a fair example of the meals here, I'll stay for the food alone.*

She studied the menu again, while sipping her tea. Nothing fancy, but if the rest was as well-cooked as tonight's steak and kidney followed by peach crumble and custard, it didn't need to be.

Finished at last, she smoothed the skirt of her apple green sundress, straightened the white jacket she had decided to wear over it, and picked up the last few items waiting to be cleared from her table. She didn't have to, but she wanted to tell Marge how much she'd enjoyed the meal, so she might as well take these things with her.

Marge's little nod of approval made her glad she did. The older woman's gentle smile widened into a proud beam of delight at Angie's words of praise.

"I've always loved cooking. Carole Tan, she and her husband have the supermarket, you know; Carole has been teaching me a few Chinese dishes. When I'm a bit more confident, I'll add them to the menu. Can you cook, Angie?"

Angie laughed ruefully. "I do a reasonable curry, but not much else. I'm so rarely home for dinner, I've never bothered about cooking."

"Maybe I could teach you." Marge cast a coy smile Angie's way.

"Maybe you could," she replied lightly. A moment later, she looked up and smiled, her green eyes sparkling with enthusiasm. "If you really mean it, Marge, I think I might enjoy learning to cook."

"Oh, I mean it," Marge answered. "You run along now, dear. I just want to finish up here, then I'm off upstairs to watch 'Law and Order'."

Dismissed from the kitchen, Angie wandered through to the bar where she ordered a lemon squash, intending to have a good look around her new domain. Her first shift was scheduled to begin the following afternoon, when she would work through to closing time with only a short break for dinner. Learning the lay of the land in advance would help her to make a good impression.

"On the house, Angie," Phil winked, then introduced her to the handful of customers. "Wednesday is usually pretty quiet," he informed her. You'll find most people hereabouts have a regular night, and stick to it."

~~~~~

Thursday night's pretty quiet, too, Angie observed the next evening, feeling lucky to have had such a leisurely first day.

During the morning, she had explored the town, pleasantly surprised to have total strangers smile and offer her a friendly 'Good morning'. She was now on first name terms with Dorothy and Sophie James from the newsagents where she had placed an order for her favourite magazines; Pete Hackett from the hardware store where she bought a pot plant for her room; and Edith Turner, the librarian, who had been a mine of information.

As well as an armful of books, she had left the library with contact details for an aerobics group and the tennis club. Tomorrow she would call them both to find out if they could fit her in. A long walk along the creek had given her an appetite for the quiche and salad Marge had set in front of her at lunchtime.

It was early days yet. However, she was already feeling quietly confident. Coming to Oxley Crossing was the best move she'd made in a very long time; an impression further reinforced when Phil took her aside after closing time. Everything was clean and tidy, ready for the next day, when he poured each of them a nightcap and sat her down at one of the tables.

"It's pretty obvious you know your way around behind the bar, Angie," he began. "How about if you handle things on your own Thursday and Monday nights, sharing duty with myself and one of our casuals on Friday, Saturday and Sunday nights. That leaves you most of every day free. Off on Tuesdays and Wednesdays."

The proposed schedule suited Angie just fine, and she didn't hesitate to say so.

"Good. Any time you want to swap a shift for any reason, let me know. There are dances around the corner in the School of Arts Hall once a month. You might enjoy them." His eyes twinkled.

"Don't let yourself get bored here in The Crossing, Angie. Country living is fine, but young people need a bit of fun now and then. I'd rather give you a few extra days off every once in a while, to kick your heels up in the Big Smoke, than go through all the rigmarole of replacing you because you were bored."

It was a long speech for Phil, whom she had discovered was more of a listener than a talker. She was happy to find him so considerate.

"You're a good girl, Angie." Patting her on the shoulder, Phil picked up their empty glasses and put them in the dishwasher.

"Goodnight, Phil," Angie called, "I think I'm going to like working for you and Marge."

Phil chuckled, returning her goodnight, and adding an amused rider. "Have a nap before you come on tomorrow, girl. Friday night gets a bit busy most weeks."

Angie wondered how busy was 'busy' in Oxley Crossing where life was lived at a leisurely pace unheard of in the city.

~~~~~

Very busy. Hectic, in fact, she decided the next evening.

From half past three when a contingent of teachers from the Central School on the edge of town, had arrived en masse to celebrate the end of the week, joined soon after by the employees of the local sawmill and timber yard, 'The Victoria's' bar had been quite lively.

She hadn't had the dining room to herself, either. Several of the afternoon's customers had eaten there before leaving, and a few early arrivals heralding the evening crowd had also savoured Marge's good cooking. By eight o'clock, she was being run off her feet.

"Hey, Angie, how about a dance?" The jukebox had been playing continuously for some time, and a rowdy group of young people were dancing nearby.

Not Tall, Dark and Handsome, though, Angie noted.

She hadn't seen him arrive, but glancing up from the till after making change, she'd noticed him watching her intently from the far corner of the bar.

He occupied the stool next to Pete Hackett whom she already knew. Since becoming aware of him, she'd felt his eyes following her about the room. He couldn't be paying too much attention to Pete's conversation, she thought, not the way he was watching *her*.

She unloaded the tray of drinks she had just delivered, and accepted payment, smiling impersonally at the slightly tipsy young man who had invited her to dance.

"Love to Joey, only I'm on duty," she returned, making a mental note to keep an eye on him. Pubs were for drinking, but the law was clear-cut on the issue of responsible service of alcohol. Joey had about reached his limit.

Out of the corner of her eye, she noticed one of a party of young women stroll over to Tall, Dark and Handsome, an exaggerated swing of her hips drawing attention to her shapely derriere. The girl threw both arms around his neck and leaned forward, brushing her breasts across his broad chest.

She was met by a cynical twist of those well-shaped masculine lips and a sharp rap on her jeans-clad bottom which caused her to draw away slightly with a discontented pout. Angie felt herself assailed by unaccustomed disgust at the unknown girl's blatant play for the man, and turned her back on the pair of them.

Collecting a new tray of drinks, she let her eyes stray casually towards the couple who'd attracted her attention. This time, her eyes meshed with the man's. Without looking away from her, he spoke to the girl, who immediately flounced off in high dudgeon. This time his cynical twist of the lips was directed challengingly at Angie.

Tossing her head as if to swing her shoulder-length curls out of her eyes, she picked up her tray and walked in the opposite direction.

Carefully *not* flouncing. Smiling cheerfully, she parried several young chaps who sought to detain her. Returning to the bar, she ducked between two parties, almost running slap-bang into her nemesis.

"Why, Angie Darlin'," he drawled, oozing seduction, "you ought to watch your step."

Blue, she thought incoherently. *His eyes are blue. Dark blue.* She hadn't even realised she'd been wondering about their colour.

Those dark blue eyes locked onto her vivid green ones as if they were the only two people in the room. He bent his head towards her, lips so close to her own she could feel the warmth of his breath. Mesmerised, she felt his hands on her hips as he steered her adroitly past himself and Pete with a bit of nimble footwork that wouldn't have been out of place on the dancefloor.

Gathering her scattered wits, Angie stepped out of what was perilously close to being an embrace, aware for one instant, she had swayed towards the broad-chested, slim-hipped, very masculine figure; rosy lips parted expectantly as she gazed up into his eyes.

Two large hands slid reluctantly from her hips and the cynicism disappeared from his face. Blue eyes alight with an expression she thought might be tenderness, his mobile lips parted in a sweetly intimate smile.

"Talk to you later, Angie," he whispered, then moved on, following Pete Hackett to the pool tables in the next room.

The whole incident was compressed within the frame of a few seconds, yet Angie felt an eternity had passed. Shaken to the core, she wondered who he was.

One thing's for sure, she told herself, *I've never met anyone like him before.*

No man she'd ever met had made such an instantaneous impact on her senses. She didn't know what to think. A tiny voice in the back of her mind whispered that he had the power to play an important role in her life. If he chose to.

For good or evil? She wondered.

She kept a wary eye on him till he left. Without coming anywhere near her again for the promised talk. Recalling her previous disappointments with men, Angie wasn't sure whether to be glad or sorry about that.

4

'Tall, Dark and Handsome' was still at the forefront of Angie's mind when she woke on Saturday morning.

Although, she thought, wrinkling her nose as she considered the matter, *handsome doesn't seem the right word, somehow. Too bland. His features are a bit too irregular for handsome. Presence. Better,* she decided.

The man had presence; and then some. And character. A frown gathered while she pondered. *Character, certainly; but is it good or bad?* She shrugged, reaching for her robe and padding barefoot across the corridor to her almost private bathroom.

Could be, the disturbing man was merely passing through, in which case she might never see him again. *Either way, only the future can tell.*

Reminding herself of her recent vow, to put her future career goals first, she tossed her head and stepped under the shower.

Relaxed, and slightly euphoric from a solid workout in the pool, Angie dawdled down the street. Not a brilliant swimmer by any means, she had doggedly persevered until she'd clocked up a respectable kilometre; well and truly earning the French pastry and hot chocolate from the Tan's bakery-café with which she had bribed herself.

Outside the stock and station agents on the corner, which doubled as the local hardware store, Pete Hackett had edged his fork-lift alongside a mud-splashed white, dual-cab ute, effectively blocking the footpath. Wondering idly why, with the plethora of lovely colours available, farmers seemed to prefer the ubiquitous white, she detoured into the craft shop while she waited for the way to clear. She could have stepped out into the road and gone round, but why bother, when the craft shop was on her schedule anyway?

After happily spending a quarter of an hour browsing around the displays, she found she'd timed it just right. The fork-lift was trundling through the gate into its yard, leaving the footpath clear again when she emerged into the sunshine.

"Why, Angie Darlin'. What an unexpected pleasure."

The remembered silky baritone, the one which had haunted her dreams, brought Angie to a halt next to the ute. A delicious frisson tingled its way down her spine as the tall, lean, very masculine figure uncoiled itself, straightening from stowing paperwork in the glovebox, to stand squarely in front of her. "You're just in time to join me for a coffee at Tan's. Shall we go?"

A calloused, long-fingered hand slid around the back of her waist, obviously intending to steer her across the street.

Except that Angie stepped aside, tossing her head to show her disdain at such presumption.

"Whoa. You're going a bit fast there, Mr ...?" Angie fluttered a hand to emphasise the inquiry. "I make it a firm practice never to accept coffee from strangers." She turned away, indicating half-hearted reluctance.

"Strangers!" The conscienceless reprobate chided her in a mournful tone. "How can you call us strangers, Angie darlin'? Not after last night when you fell into my arms like a dove coming home to roost. A most beautiful dove," he added, silent laughter crinkling the corners of dancing blue eyes, wide, sensuous lips twitching; inviting her to share his nonsense.

"A ridiculous exaggeration," she scoffed, frowning her resistance to the serious temptation he posed. A practised charmer, she didn't need!

"Utter delusion!" she added for good measure, taking another prudent, backward step. The unrepentant rogue followed her, practically pinning her against the side of his ute.

"Angie." The mock-mournful tone was back, adding to her irritation. You really don't know my name? Anyone in the pub last night could have told you."

"If I'd been sufficiently interested to ask." Feigned indifference aside, Angie discovered she was enjoying herself hugely.

"Oh, you were interested all right," he grinned, "You couldn't take your eyes off me."

The conceit of the man.

Angie almost gasped aloud.

The smooth voice deepened a notch, the head tilting forward until Angie's face was shaded by the brim of the battered black Akubra. "Any more than I could take my eyes off you. *I* was interested, Angie. *I* learned a whole lot about you."

Fingers threaded gently through Angie's bright curls, separating the strands set ablaze by sunlight streaming down across his shoulder. Serious now, he whispered, almost to himself.

"A living flame to set fire to a man's heart." Releasing her hair, he ran the back of his hand across her cheek in a lingering caress. A sigh puffed from those tempting male lips.

Moved, despite her instinctive distrust, Angie stood transfixed. Then the moment was gone. Straightening, he stepped back, the irrepressible grin returning. Extending his right hand in invitation, he jauntily identified himself.

"Alan Morgan, of 'Morgan's Run'."

"Angelica Wilson, temporarily of 'The Victoria Inn'." The touch of sarcasm helped her keep her equilibrium as she placed her hand in his; startled when he lifted it to his lips instead of shaking it as she'd expected. Eyes challenging, he brushed a kiss across the back of her wrist.

"A tribute to beauty," he murmured.

Beginning to feel a little out of her depth, Angie floundered through a morass of disconnected thoughts, rescue finally coming from an unexpected source. Hot breath fanned across her cheek, startling her anew. Whipping round, she found herself nose-to-nose with a furry face sporting a pair of intelligent brown eyes.

A sloppy, pink tongue lolled from a doggy grin Angie considered to be remarkably like its master's. A brown paw swung confidently above the side of the ute. With a wordless exclamation of delight, Angie accepted the invitation.

"Morgana-le-Fey. Fey for short," Alan introduced the engaging young kelpie.

"Hungry dog," Angie commented, silently counting the stacked cartons and sacks of dog food filling the bed of the ute, leaving precious little room for the dog.

"One of many," Alan told her. "Dad breeds and trains kelpies. Their awards and trophies cover the walls of his study. My meagre contribution from school days are hidden away in the back of a cupboard. But then, I never made State Champion, let alone National. Or Best of Breed, either."

She laughed at his whimsy.

"Second-rate, are you? Couldn't make the grade. I guess it might be inappropriate to call you a son-of-a-bitch, then," Angie commiserated, straight-faced.

A crack of laughter registered her hit, although it had been touch and go. For a split second the sparkling blue eyes had narrowed into steely glints of outraged male ego.

"One day, Angelica Wilson! One day you'll get yours." Rueful, Alan shook his head, committing the joke to memory to share with his father. The Old Man would get a kick out of it, he reckoned.

"Now you're threatening me." All scorn again, she tossed her curls, pert nose elevated.

"Promises, Angie Darlin'. Promises, not threats." Alan took her arm and headed across the street. "Now that we've been introduced all round, let's grab that coffee. If we hurry up, we can beat that bus-load of oldies bearing down on Tan's."

"Okay." Angie acquiesced, although not without one last shot. "But only because Morgana-le-Fey vouched for you. Her, I trust."

~~~~~

Two days passed before Angie heard from Alan Morgan again. They had lingered over their coffee, parting without either of them mentioning a future meeting. His nonsense aside, he had turned out to be a thoroughly likeable man. One Angie really would enjoy seeing more of.

Soon.

"Phone, Angie," Marge called through the window to where Angie had ensconced herself in the sunny garden with her laptop, to catch up on her latest assignment for TAFE.

"A very self-confident young man is asking to speak to Angelica Wilson," she added, exiting the room to allow Angie to take the call in private. Her heart sped up as she reached for the phone.

Only one man in Oxley Crossing knew her as Angelica.

"Angelica Wilson speaking." She refused to give free reign to the excitement welling up within her.

"Very formal today, aren't you Angie Darlin'?" intoned the now familiar drawl, its hint of laughter coaxing a chuckle from her.

"You too. No-one ever calls me Angelica. I'm too down to earth for fancy names. Never did figure out what Mum was thinking to saddle me with it."

"Oh, I don't know, I reckon it kind of suits you Angie darlin'. You're one fancy lady." Voice changing, Alan briskly came to the point.

"Tomorrow's your day off, according to my information. Got any plans? Because if you haven't, I can wangle a couple of hours off. How about letting me show you the sights? I'll even throw in a picnic lunch."

"Sounds good." She pretended nonchalance, and, quickly agreeing on time, hung up first.

The lilt in her voice matched the smile on her face as she informed Marge of her date. It was hard to settle back to writing her essay with rosy daydreams filling her mind. *Career first*, she counselled herself, but that still left plenty of time to explore other possibilities; especially ones contained in such an attractive package.

~~~~~

In an unaccustomed dither, Angie changed her mind three times over what to wear on her date with Alan Morgan.

Construing her state of mind, so different to her usual pragmatic self, as a warning from the Gods, she sat down and purposefully forced herself to make a realistic assessment, ticking off the facts on her fingers.

Item: Alan Morgan is one very attractive man, but not the first one I've been out with, So, why is he getting to me like this?

Item: It can't be love. I've been in love before, and it doesn't feel like this, or arise so quickly. Besides, I don't want to fall in love; it never lasts, and leaves me feeling horrible.

A flashback to her affair with Luke Freeman helped cool her emotions. What she was experiencing must be a violent infatuation. A flash in the pan, then all over. With a sour grimace Angie continued compiling her list.

Item: Men can't be trusted. That Alan is attracted to me doesn't mean much. I'm new in town, and pretty enough to catch his eye. He's obviously an experienced flirt, and will be off as soon as someone else arrives on the scene.

Item: We're only going for a drive and a picnic, so jeans, a cool top and comfortable walking shoes will be eminently practical. A hat, too. And if I don't hurry up, I'll be late.

She glanced at her watch, and finished getting dressed. Walking down the main staircase a while later, she appeared so coolly self-possessed no-one would have credited her earlier, turbulent mood.

"Alan," she greeted the man leaning placidly against the newel post with an air of casual pleasure, glad to see *he* was the one doing the waiting. "How lovely to see you again. I do hope I haven't kept you waiting."

"Angelica Dearest, your delightful company is reward enough, even had I to wait an eternity."

Marge's giggle reminded them both they were in a public space, the red tinge warming the outdoor bronze of Alan's cheeks drawing a complacent smirk form his lady fair.

"Such gallantry," Marge sighed. "I never knew you had it in you to play the romantic, Alan Morgan. You know, Angie, I rather like the sound of Angelica. Such a pretty name."

Angie laughed. Saying their goodbyes, they hurried out to the ute.

"No mud!" she exclaimed, pleased and surprised to observe its white paint sparkling and clean.

"I even vacuumed the cab. Just for you, Angie Darlin'," He pointed out with a smug grin as he helped her into the passenger seat. Shared laughter floated through the open window as they drove off, setting the tone for the rest of the day.

Their driving tour had eventually brought them to the lookout on top of One Tree Hill. Taking the picnic basket and rug in one hand, the other firmly clasping Angie's, Alan led her up a gravel path to the rocky outcrop on the summit.

The tree from which the hill derived its name, an ancient, gnarled eucalypt, cast lacy shade over a tiny patch of grass at the base of a huge granite boulder, ideally sited to act as a windbreak.

"What a magnificent view, Alan. I wish I'd thought to bring my camera."

"Next time," Alan promised, the intimation of future outings causing joy to infuse Angie's heart, and set it beating a little faster.

"Now, woman, sit down and eat. I'm starving." A prosaic enough statement to bring her back to earth. Delving into the insulated basket, he handed her cold chicken salad rolls and chilled fruit juice.

"Hope you like my selection," he said, Passing her a couple of paper napkins. "There's chocolate brownies for desert."

A feast. Impulsively, Angie leaned over and planted a soft kiss on Alan's cheek. "Thank you for a lovely morning, Alan."

Blushing, she turned her eyes to the view, not sure her gesture had been appreciated, and missed the arrested look on Alan's face. A look which melted into a caressing warmth.

"The day's not over yet," he whispered. Hunger forgotten, he returned her kiss, full on her rosy lips. A gently questing, exploratory kiss.

Arms creeping up to encircle Alan's neck, Angie gave in to the temptation she'd been fighting for the last hour. Her lips parted under the probing sweep of his tongue, allowing him entry to the honeyed sweetness of her mouth.

They became lost in the excitement of mutual passion. Mad urgency gentled into something altogether sweeter, and even more compelling. Alan pressed Angie down onto the rug. Blue eyes drugged with desire, he traced the planes of her face; first with work-roughened fingers, then soothing the light abrasiveness with warm lips, softer than the brush of a butterfly's wing.

"So lovely, Angie Darlin'. So lovely," he murmured. "Such white skin, and those beautiful emerald eyes, all wrapped around in a sunset blaze of curls." His mouth claimed another kiss, slower and deeper than the previous wild onslaught. Tongue stroked tongue with erotic promises.

Passion drugging her senses, Angie set her hands free, exploring the shapes and textures of male muscle and bone. Fingers threaded through thick, dark waves, drawing Alan into her warmth.

Moist kisses nibbling the tender length of her throat, probing the delicate hollows of her clavicle, elicited a shuddering response. Her hands drew him back to her hungry mouth, demanding more of those soul-searing kisses.

Alan's hands stroked their way over her shoulders and arms; down to her slender waist. Inching higher, they circled her full breasts, cupping them in warm palms, thumbs teasing sensitive nipples into hard, erect peaks through the concealing garments. Angie's purring satisfaction incited Alan to trail his lips into the shadowy valley between, and across the mounded tops.

The feel of fabric being pushed ruthlessly aside penetrated Angie's passion-haze; stilling the sensuous movements of her hands and body. Feeling her unresponsive stillness, Alan lifted his head, glazed eyes studying her intently.

"Angie? What's the matter, Darlin'?" he questioned softly.

She raised herself from her supine position, wriggling out from beneath his intoxicating nearness, until she was sitting once again. Avoiding his too-knowing eyes, she straightened her clothes with nervous hands.

Gentle fingers under her chin, Alan turned her face towards him, concern etched upon his strained features.

"Angie?" he whispered again.

A shattered expression on her face, Angie opened her eyes, meeting his; drowning in their emotion darkened depths.

"Oh Alan," she breathed. "I'm so sorry. It's just …" She struggled to find the right words.

"Too soon?" Grateful for his understanding, she nodded her head.

"Much too soon," she agreed. "Everything's been going so fast, it's hard to believe we barely know each other."

And yet I want him, she thought, her body yearning to return to his heady embrace. *I want him unbearably.* It was only her mind throwing up barriers.

Alan wrapped comforting arms around her. Pressing her head onto his shoulder, he rocked her like a child in his arms, soothing her distress.

"It's okay," he assured her. "It's okay, Angie Darlin'. I got a bit carried away, but I'm okay now."

Relieved, she moved out of his arms, a tentative smile turning up the corners of her mouth. Alan let her have her way, until his light grip was holding her at arms' length.

"I'm telling you, Angie. I want you. More than I've wanted any woman in a very long while. I'm not giving up on us, you understand; only, when we make love, it's going to be because you want me every bit as much as I want you. No reservations. No holding back."

Emerald eyes locked on blue, Angie longed to give in to the desire still roiling through her veins. Only … She had been right to call a halt. For all his power to arouse her to passion, Alan Morgan *was* still little more than a stranger. She focused her attention on what he was saying.

"It won't be easy, Angie, but I can wait till then," he concluded.

Wicked grin flashing, he swooped in for a last, quick, hard kiss; then picked up her forgotten lunch. Handing her the roll, he reached for his own. "Eat up, or you'll miss out. Frustrated lust makes me hungry enough to clear the basket on my own." He cast a considering gaze towards the sky. "We'll have to be going soon, anyway."

A lightning flash, quickly followed by a rumble of thunder, supported his statement. While they'd been engrossed with each other, a predicted front had rolled west across The Divide, an afternoon storm in its wake. By the time they arrived back in The Crossing, a chilly rain was falling. Sitting, chatting in the cab till the worst of the storm passed, Alan turned to Angie, taking her hand in both of his.

"I'm going to be tied up for the next few days, Angie, but there's a dance on at the Hall Saturday night. Do you think Phil would give you the night off? I'd love to dance with you," he cajoled.

"I think so." Angie brightened at the thought. She did enjoy dancing, and with Alan … It would be so romantic. "Phil mentioned the dances, and said I could swap shifts if I wanted to go."

"Good ol' Phil." A slow, satisfied smile stole across Alan's face. "Ask him. I'll ring you Friday. Give me your number so I don't have to go through Marge again."

The rain having almost stopped, he raced Angie across to the hotel's door, kissed her quickly, then departed with a wave of his hand through the driver's window.

5

On Friday, Angie was walking on air, her phone in her pocket everywhere she went.

He only said Friday, she reminded herself. *No indication of exactly when. Oh, I can't wait to hear his voice again*. Phil had raised no objections when she asked, merely asking her to do the day shift instead.

Collecting her exercise mat, she set off for her pump class, looking forward to seeing the friendly group of young women, almost as much as the energetic workout itself. Unlike the gym in Sydney, exercise classes in The Crossing were a social event, participants usually adjourning to Tan's for coffee and cake and a catch-up on the local gossip.

Today, Rhonda Molinar was passing around a packet of photos taken on her son's recent school excursion.

"Hey Ang," she flipped one across the table, "here's one you might find interesting."

Leaning over, Rhonda pointed out, first her own handsome youngster, then a pretty little girl sporting a mop of dark curls and an oddly familiar, pert grin. Angie looked up, puzzled. She hadn't got to know any of the kids around town yet.

"That's Jocelyn Morgan, Alan's youngest," Rhonda elucidated "A real chip off the old block, isn't she?"

Angie's heart dropped like a stone, her mind reeling.

Alan's daughter? His youngest! How many children has he got? She thought wildly. And what about their mother? His wife!

She didn't know how she managed not to give herself away. The conversation moved on to another topic, and she made her escape soon after, her mind still in a whirl.

Alan Morgan was a married man!

Thank goodness, I called a halt the other day. She made it a strict rule not to get involved with married men.

Alan Bloody Morgan had some explaining to do. Although, when she got over the initial shock, common sense came creeping back. If he *was* married, surely Marge, or even one of the girls, today, would have warned her. Certainly, Marge would have.

Even so, she argued with herself, *he hasn't been straight with me. He's still got some explaining to do.*

∿∿∿∿∿

Angie's feet ached, and she longingly eyed the row of chairs along the side of the dancefloor.

On entering the Hall, she'd been swept into a crowd of young people, most of whom she'd met in the bar, all intent on having an enjoyable time.

When Alan finally rang that afternoon, it was to say he was going to be late getting into town. She should go to the dance on her own, and he'd meet her there as soon as he could. A pity, she fumed. Now she couldn't get him on his own for that much-needed private conversation, till the dance was over.

Maybe not so bad, she mused. If he *was* off-limits, she didn't want to stir up gossip by arriving on his arm.

"You're not working now, Angie, so how about that dance you owe me?"

"Joey. Of course," she smiled at the lanky young timber-cutter, allowing him to swing her onto the floor as the band struck up for the first set. From then on, she passed from partner to partner, barely given time to catch her breath.

The band had already taken their first break and were into their second session. No wonder her feet ached, especially since she was wearing the near-new four-inch stilettos which did such wonderful things for her legs.

Then she looked up to see Alan coming through the door. Edging his way through the crowd, eyes skimming boldly over the sophisticated picture she made in her very short, silver halter dress, heels and upswept hair, he was waiting for her when the dance ended.

"Evening, Angie Darlin'," he drawled. "You're looking mighty fine tonight."

"Alan," she smiled at him, hoping the heat she felt rising in her cheeks would be attributed to her exertions on the dancefloor. "You made it then. I was beginning to think you must have changed your mind."

"I'm not all that late, Angie, and I did warn you I couldn't make it on time."

"So you did."

The music started up again. Alan made to lead her onto the floor, only to find himself being rudely elbowed aside. "Wait your turn, Morgan. This is my dance. Angie promised."

"I did," she corroborated. "Sorry Alan. The next one's yours." *Tough!* She thought, smiling limpidly. Ignoring his thunderous scowl. She was secretly delighted to have an excuse to put him in his place. Alan Morgan didn't own her; and until he came clean, she wasn't cutting him any slack.

"Arrive late, you miss out," gloated her new partner.

In the end, Alan only scored two dances with her, although both were highly coveted slow numbers she'd made a point of saving for him. It was a tacit agreement at these dances, that no girl be left a wallflower. Even so, there was no denying Angie Wilson was the belle of the ball tonight. Except for Alan, she danced every dance with a different partner.

Even the imposing police sergeant, Don Matthews, and old 'Doc' Rogers aiding and abetting each other in stealing her away from her more youthful admirers, had scored a dance apiece.

The anthem played at last, signalling the end of festivities, and Alan bustled Angie away with all speed, a glare warning off anyone with different ideas.

"Do you mind if we walk in the park awhile?" she asked. "We haven't had a minute to ourselves to just talk."

After being forced to share her with half the male population of the north-west, Alan was all in favour of getting Angie to himself, but something in her tone warned him her mind wasn't running along the amorous lines his was.

Dusting off the secluded park bench he'd chosen, he stole a kiss as they sat down. When Angie drew back, he stifled a sigh. *Why couldn't I have chosen a less prickly girl?* Keeping one small, capable hand tucked between both of his large, calloused palms, he gave in.

"Okay, Angie Darlin'. Whatever you've got on your mind, let's have it. Then, maybe we can find something more interesting to do than talk."

Angie took a moment or two to compose her thoughts before complying with the first of his commands. The second would rely entirely on his response. She was quite firm about that.

"You haven't been straight with me, Alan," she stated, with no room for prevarication. "I don't say you've lied; merely that you haven't been up front. Just hear me out," she demanded, when he would have interrupted.

"I'm not one for gossip, and I've not asked anyone else to fill me in. I prefer to deal with you directly, but I can't help hearing what's said in my presence. You've got kids, Alan, which implies a wife. I have a strict policy. I don't get involved with married men. Never."

Tugging her hand free, she stopped a now grim looking man from speaking. His turn would come, and she wanted to get this off her chest as quickly as possible.

"Since Marge didn't warn me off, I must assume you qualify as a free man; but you should have told me, yourself, Alan. You had time and opportunity the other day. Now I'm asking you to explain, rather than force me to go behind your back for answers."

An unpleasant, sarcastic tone coloured his answer. "Are you sure you trust me tell you the truth?" Alan snapped out. He was annoyed with her, and let it show.

Angie stared him down, her implacable expression clearly visible in the dim wash of distant streetlights. Only when he finally looked away, did she speak.

"If I didn't trust you, I wouldn't be here. That's another of my rules for survival, Alan. I don't date anyone I don't trust. This just goes to show how right I was the other day. We simply don't know each other well enough, do we? Hearing about your kids shook me up a bit, and I don't like nasty surprises."

Mollified, Alan relaxed a little. Although still tense, he was no longer so angry. Eyes dead ahead, he clasped his hands between his knees, reciting a litany of personal data in a flat, impersonal tone.

Angie's words had struck home. A stranger in town, she couldn't be expected to know what was common knowledge to everyone else. Despite his initial flare of temper, he was impressed she had come to him, instead of listening to the gossips, with whom Oxley Crossing was plentifully endowed.

"The banks were giving Dad a hard time when I finished school," he began, "So I stayed home where I was needed. Signed on as an external student to get my degree. Wasn't much fun, working on the farm from daylight to dusk, then slogging away at the books half the night."

Angie nodded. Studying via the same mode, she understood perfectly.

"It took me quite a while. When I was close to the end, things had improved, and Dad was able to give me my final year on campus. I guess I went a bit overboard with the partying. One night I met Janice at a uni do. We hit it off and started running around together. Her family are high flyers. Property developers. I guess she was slumming with me, a farm boy from the back of beyond. We got a bit careless, and next thing I knew, she was pregnant. I persuaded her to marry me. I wanted my kid."

He shrugged, and Angie suspected there was probably a whole lot more to the story than the bare bones she was hearing.

"We ended up with two kids, Melanie, then Jocelyn a couple of years later. Janice stuck it out a bit longer, even though she loathed the bush. Eventually, she left the girls with me and high-tailed it back to the bright lights; and the nearest divorce lawyer." He sat up, finally turning to look Angie in the face.

"There you have it, Angelica."

"I thought it had to be something along those lines," Angie observed. "It was the not knowing; the possibility I was being played for a fool, that threw me."

She planted an apologetic kiss on his cheek. "Thank you for bearing with me, Alan," she whispered.

He put his arm round her shoulders, tucking her in against his side. For a minute, he simply stared morosely into the night, lost in bitter memories evoked by the enforced confrontation with the ghosts from his past.

What is it with me, he questioned. *After Janice, anyone would think I'd have the good sense to steer clear of city girls; yet here I am with another one. Just setting myself up for another fall.* His lips tightened grimly as he followed that thought through. *Difference is, I know better than to get caught again. No serious involvements for me. Not again.*

Women were easy to find when his body demanded release; and that was his only use for them. Although he usually did his looking further afield than The Crossing, he felt confident he'd be safe with his pretty little barmaid.

A townie, she wouldn't stay long; and in the meantime, all a woman of her type would be looking for was a good time. He became aware of Angie's soft weight leaning against him.

And a good time is what we'll both be having.

He pulled Angie onto his lap and proceeded to kiss her breathless. Until she stiffened, and pushed away from him. "Still too soon, is it?" There was the trace of a sneer in his voice. He stood her on her feet, and rose.

Looked like the good time was still on hold while she played her game of pretending to be hard to get. "Come on Angie, I'll walk you home This evening hasn't exactly gone the way I envisaged it."

"And I suppose you reckon it's all my fault." Disgruntled, she refused to shoulder the blame. He shouldn't have needed prodding. Arriving at the side door Marge had given her a key to, she turned to say goodnight.

"Will I be seeing you again?" Her careless tone implied it didn't matter either way.

Alan stared at her for a long moment, eyes hard as flint.

"Oh, yes, Angie Darlin'." The caressing velvety timbre was back in his voice, she noted. "You'll be seeing me just as often as I can arrange it. Starting Monday. Lunch would be nice, don't you think?"

Lunch was less than he wanted, but he'd lost a lot of ground tonight, and he'd be damned if he let her go so someone else could snap up the tastiest prize in the offing.

Angie Wilson was his.

"As long as I'm behind the bar by two," Angie agreed, more relieved than she had any intention of letting on. Alan Morgan had gotten under her skin in a way no-one else ever had.

She reached up, pulling his head down for her kiss. And this time, *she* set the pace, beginning to end.

Difficult bloody-minded male that he was, Alan Morgan was going to be hers.

On her terms.

6

From her table in Tan's courtyard, Angie watched Alan across the street, loading drums and boxes sporting interesting looking labels, into the back of his ute.

Swallowing hard, she admired the play of muscles stretching his shirt taut across back and chest. Tight jeans strained at the seams as he bent to hoist the last drum. Palms itching to explore his lithe, slim-hipped body, she squirmed in her chair.

How she wanted that man!

The searing intensity of her desire took her by surprise. She'd known, desired, even loved, other men; however, her feelings for Alan Morgan surpassed all. Not only surpassed, but were inexplicably different, making her feel vulnerable.

She was entering new territory here. Eager anticipation see-sawed for supremacy with trepidation, and she warned herself to guard her heart.

Heart racing, Angie tracked his approach, composing her features to disguise her uncomfortable thoughts.

"Hey, Angie Darlin'. Sorry to keep you waiting, but it's business before pleasure, you know. And you are my pleasure, woman," Alan growled, one knuckle intimately caressing her cheek while bold blue eyes told her his greeting would have been considerably more physical if they'd been alone.

Heartened by the lambert green fire blazing from Angie's eyes, contradicting her prim response, Alan leaned closer, so only she could hear; his high-voltage smile coaxing an answering, though more tentative, smile from those enticing, moist, red lips.

"Come on, Angelica," he commanded. "You can do better than that. Tell me how much you've missed me."

The last of her reservations temporarily melting in blue flames mirroring her own desire, Angie threw caution to the wind, a joyous peal of laughter attracting admiring glances from the handful of other people sharing the sunny courtyard.

"I've been missing you just as much as you've been missing me; and that's forever."

She was uttering the truth, she realised, at least regarding herself. She wasn't too sure how they applied to Alan, but her words were no facetious playacting.

"You, Alan Morgan, are the missing ingredient to make my life complete."

She wasn't sure how Alan would take her effusive reply, so the arrival of Elizabeth Tan to take their order, was a welcome distraction.

Always quick to scent romance in the air, Elizabeth lingered, teasing Alan and giving Angie time to take herself in hand. Her relationship with Alan was too new, too uncertain, for voicing such profound truths.

Falling back on well-rehearsed professional banter, she flirted outrageously throughout the meal, refusing to behave seriously, and thought she'd probably got away with it.

The flirtatious nonsense suited Alan's mood perfectly. For one stomach-lurching moment he'd thought Angie was speaking from the heart, and had been mentally scrabbling to put together an excuse to high-tail it out of town, never to return. At least not to anywhere in Angie Wilson's vicinity. He had seized on Elizabeth's timely interruption, relieved on sneaking a sidelong glance across the table, to catch Angie laughing at him.

The witch, he thought ruefully, *she was winding me up*. That was a game two could play. Impudently, he set out to charm her all over again with his arrantly provocative nonsense.

It had been amusing, this flirty badinage, Alan thought, restlessly checking his watch, except now his frustration level was higher than ever.

Next time he'd plan better, to ensure they had privacy. He desperately needed to exchange words for deeds. Shifting in his chair, he eased the pressure of constricting jeans on a delicate portion of his anatomy.

When Alan looked at his watch, Angie glanced at her own. Time was almost up, and she didn't want to say goodbye in this public place.

Casting about for a ploy to get him to herself, she spied the large cardboard carton on the empty chair, her handbag flung down carelessly on top of it, and was struck by inspiration. Deliberately leaning across the table letting Alan catch a tantalising eyeful of her cleavage, she smugly noted the effect it had on him.

"Alan," she lowered her voice into a sultry Mae West imitation. "Want to come up to my room, big boy?"

"Lead me to it, Angie Darlin'," he responded promptly. "Although I do wish you'd made this offer earlier. We're going to be a bit rushed, if you want to be on time for work. I'd dreamed of taking my time with you when I finally got you into a room with a bed."

His smug, self-satisfied smirk was arrested by Angie's reaction.

Walking round the table to stand close beside him, she cupped his face in one soft hand, the other gripping his chair behind his shoulders. Mimicking his manner, she paraphrased his speech to her from their first date, and then some.

"Alan Darlin'," she purred, "I want you. More than I've wanted any man in a very long time. I want to make love to you; no reservations; no holding back. And when I do, I'm going to take my time over it. No rushing. I can wait till then"

Patting his cheek, she stepped back slowly, head erect, spine straight, maintaining eye contact.

Now the self-satisfied smirk was on her face.

"Now, Alan Darlin', pick that up," she pointed to the carton, "and make out it's as heavy as the ones in your ute so Marge thinks you're merely being gentlemanly and helping me out."

Laughing, he slipped a note out of his wallet, anchoring it under his plate, to pay for their lunch, picked up the carton as ordered, and lengthened his stride to catch up with the red-haired temptress sashaying down the street towards 'The Victoria'.

"What's in it, anyway?" he asked. It was so light he was going to have to put on an award-winning act to make it appear heavy.

"Not much," Angie grinned, dropping her femme fatale pose. "Just some things I picked up from St Vinnie's. The fabrics are beautiful. I'll unpick them and make up fancy cushion covers. Sewing's one of my hobbies."

Their ruse worked. "Can't stop to chat, Marge," Alan hailed with cheeky insouciance, "Madam here is running late and is too frail to lug this upstairs for herself."

~~~~~

Hesitating in the doorway to Angie's room, Alan silently observed the homely touches with which she had transformed the impersonal hotel room into a cosy feminine retreat.

A voracious reader, she had books stacked on the bedside tables and small writing desk; their titles ranging from novels of all genres, to poetry and biographies, indicative of her eclectic interests.

Her original potplant had multiplied into a small jungle, covering the full width of her windowsill, and a bright patchwork quilt and scatter cushions had replaced the original pink chenille bedcover.

"Your work, Angie?" Alan gestured towards the quilt, letting his curious eyes rove around Angie's domain. It wasn't at all what he'd expected.

"That's right. Dump the box in the corner." Angie closed the door, and when Alan straightened, she was close behind him. Sliding her arms around his waist as he turned towards her, she rose on tip-toes to meet his impatient lips half-way.

"I'm glad I thought of a way to slip you past Marge. I wanted to kiss you so badly, I felt I'd die if I couldn't get you to myself."

"Me too," he whispered back. "I'd about reconciled myself to waiting till tomorrow."

"Tomorrow?"

"Mmm ..." Alan kissed her again, running one hand up and down her spine; the other kneading her shapely bottom, pressing her against the hard bulge rendering his jeans uncomfortable.

"Tomorrow is your day off, isn't it? You have your own key, don't you? Marge won't wait up, will she?" Angie nodded yes to the lot. "Then I know a great place we can wine and dine, and afterwards we can take all the time we need to keep the promises we made earlier."

The grandfather clock in the lower hallway chimed the third quarter, reminding Angie she still had to change for work.

Reluctantly, she dragged herself out of Alan's arms. "It's a date," she stated calmly, reaching up for one last kiss. "And Alan? You know what they say, don't you? If it's not on, it's not on."

"Not very romantic, are you Angie?" Although he had every intention of taking precautions, he was rather taken aback by her utterly prosaic attitude.

"Take care of the practicalities first, then we can be as romantic as we please," was her pragmatic reply. Noticing Alan's moue of distaste, she rounded on him smartly.

"There's no need to look at me like that, Alan Morgan. I'm a woman of *this* century, not some simpering throwback to the Victorian era. And remember, I don't like nasty surprises."

He didn't either, Alan reminded himself. He ought to be feeling grateful for her common-sense approach, instead of vaguely insulted.

"You won't catch me taking foolish risks," she continued. "Being practical doesn't mean my feelings for you are any less. The reverse, if anything."

"Yeah, I see your point, Angie Darlin', and I do appreciate your forethought. It just caught me by surprise, is all."

What had he been thinking? Getting in a snit? She'd promised him everything he wanted, hadn't she? Tomorrow. No more shilly-shallying. He ought to be cheering.

"You know, Angelica. For a woman who doesn't like surprises, you're pretty full of them yourself."

"Surely not nasty ones, Alan Dear." Angie gazed at him all wide-eyed innocence. "They're the only kind I don't like."

"No Darlin'," he chuckled. "Your surprises aren't even a little bit nasty. A bit shocking maybe, but definitely not nasty."

"Right. Now get out of here. I still have to change and get downstairs in the next couple of minutes."

"Sure I can't help? I'm very experienced with zips and buttons." His confident grin was back in evidence.

"I'm sure you are. I'm equally sure I'll be quicker on my own." She held the door wide. "Out."

She permitted a quick kiss, then shoved him through the door, shutting it with a bang behind him.

She couldn't help laughing while she scurried into her work clothes. She'd sure shaken that arrogant bloke up a bit in the last ten minutes.

Do him good. He needn't think he'll be getting everything his own way from here on, either. Men need to be reminded occasionally that modern women expect equality, even in the bedroom.

Especially the cocky ones like Alan Morgan.

It shouldn't make any difference that I was the one to take the initiative today.

7

Perched on a stool by the breakfast bar, a glass of red wine, from which she sipped from time to time, in one hand, dainty manicured feet in strappy black sandals oscillating idly in space, Angie studied the man chopping onion and capsicum in the kitchen.

At first, when he'd turned off the bitumen onto the gravelled track, she'd assumed he was taking her to his family home for dinner; quickly realising her mistake when they pulled up in front of this modest cottage, instead of the spacious homestead she felt sure would house the Morgans of 'Morgan's Run'.

"Mum's parents built it as a retirement home," Alan had explained. "After Nan, then Pop, died a few years back, Mum started renting it out. There've been no takers for a bit, and she's looking at using it for farmstay holidays. It's likely to be vacant for a few weeks, and I reckon it's going to make an excellent hideaway for the two of us, Angie Darlin'."

Coolly assessing blue eyes dared her to disagree, warming with approval when she nodded.

She hoped his mother wouldn't be offended by his use of the house. Or take exception to herself over the use they were putting it to; but dealing with his mother was Alan's business. All she could do was wait and see.

"Ours. Our house. I like the sound of that. You've been very clever, Darling. Your place or mine, isn't really a viable option for us, is it?" His grateful kiss had been suitable reward for her compliance.

His tour of inspection once they finally made it through the front door, had been somewhat cursory, until they reached the last room.

"The master bedroom, Angelica," he opened the door with a flourish. "For the master and his mistress. More comfortable than a swag in the back of the ute, which was the second option."

He flung himself backwards onto the queen-sized bed, tugging her hand so she overbalanced, landing sprawled across his chest. "I've been looking forward all day to letting you have your wicked way with me, woman."

His words were muffled as he nibbled on her earlobe, causing her to squirm with pleasure. For a few minutes longer, she let him set the pace, then sat up. Tracing a finger over those firm lips, carefully plotting her course. She wanted a proper relationship. Sex, no matter how good, formed only one part of all she wanted with Alan.

"I've got two hungers, my Darling," she informed him, pouting as her eyes explored his uncovered chest, "and my hunger for you is likely to take a very long time to satisfy. You did promise me dinner; so, off the bed, and lead me to the dining room."

"Angie," Alan groaned, protesting. "You're a cruel woman, you know. Only, because I'm beginning to think I'll need sustenance to give me the strength to do you justice, I'll go along with you. This time."

Without warning, he flipped her over onto her back, and began tickling her ruthlessly, until he had her sobbing with laughter, and begging for mercy. Rising to his feet, he picked her up and slung her over his shoulder and strode out of the bedroom, coming to a halt in the kitchen where he set her upright, steadying her till she had her balance.

"There you are, woman. The kitchen. All yours."

"Uh-uh. No way, mister. Your invitation. Your kitchen. You cook." She didn't mind helping, but she wasn't going to let him set a precedent, expecting her to always take the lead in household tasks. Angie wanted a partnership.

An equal partnership.

Grin at its most unrepentant, Alan allowed her to grab a fistful of his shirt and steer him backwards until she had him wedged up against the sink. "Do a good job, Alan Darlin' and I'll make it worth your while." Angie pressed herself against his responsive body, pulling his head down to administer a small sample of what awaited him.

"Promises, promises, woman. That's all you're good for," he complained, when she let him up for air.

Settling herself on the stool, Angie brushed her hair back, and studied his finer points, taking her own sweet time to answer. "Feed me," she ordered, voice seductively low, "Then, you'll find out first hand, what I'm good for."

∿∿∿∿∿

Alan Morgan was quick and competent in the kitchen, Angie observed, comparing his technique to Marge's. Better than she was, at any rate. There and then, she decided to waste no time taking Marge up on her offer of cooking lessons. Alan would never let her live it down if she couldn't hold her own in the kitchen.

Also, the lessons would help if she ever realised her secret dreams for a B&B of her own.

Taking another sip of her wine, she mulled over the events of the past two days. It had felt wonderfully self-affirming, being assertive about her own needs. Very satisfying. In previous relationships, she had been relegated to a passive role, however, she had changed. Grown up, perhaps. She had definitely grown stronger.

Her strength and determination had been proven in her run-in with Max Porterman, and now she revelled in the feeling of empowerment she experienced, being mistress of her own destiny.

No longer was she being swept along, willy-nilly, by capricious fate. In Oxley Crossing she was a new woman; one making her own choices in life.

Which thought brought her full circle. Back to Alan Morgan. Eying him speculatively, she pondered on their relationship, absolutely determined not to be meek and submissive. There was a touch of arrogance about him, warning her he would walk all over her, given half a chance. Which was why she'd stood up for herself from the very beginning.

And would continue to do so; although she had no ambition to dominate him, any more than to be dominated by him. His cocky self-assurance had attracted her from the first.

I like him just as he is, she mused fondly. *What I want is to share; to be partners in the relationship growing between us.*

Partners. The word had a satisfying ring to it. *Partners in life*, she decided, carrying the idea through to its logical conclusion.

There was more to her need for Alan Morgan than mere sexual attraction; no matter how strong it was. She even found herself attracted to the idea of playing a role in the lives of his children.

Partners, she told herself again, savouring the complex textures of the relationship conjured up by that one simple word. *Equal partners*, she reminded herself.

Now that really did sound good.

Emerging from her reverie, Angie snapped back to reality. Tonight, was their beginning, her's and Alan's. They had a long road to travel together, though, before they could call themselves partners.

Leaving her wine, she went to fetch place mats and cutlery. In next to no time, Alan was seating her at the table and sliding a bowl of stir-fried chicken and cashews in front of her. Casting around in her mind for a normal, ordinary topic of conversation, she recalled the party just beginning in the bar when she was leaving tonight. At the time, it had aroused her curiosity.

"Alan Darling, who is Megan?"

"Which Megan would that be?" Alan quizzed. The only Megan he could think of had been out of town on business since about the time of Angie's arrival in The Crossing.

"The one who was pouring champagne like it was water. Slender, short brown hair, lovely grey eyes. Usually it's quiet on weeknights, but tonight half the town was in the bar. Mike Patterson from the garage was all over her, proud as a dog with two tails, and Eddie Turner was proposing a toast 'To our Megan ...'. That's how I know her name. You arrived just then, so I didn't hear any more. Do you know her?"

Angie had been intrigued by the scene in the bar, and looked inquisitively at Alan.

"Oh," he teased, drawing the moment out. "That Megan." When Angie pouted and threatened him with pretend violence, he capitulated.

"She's Megan Patterson, Mike's daughter. I didn't know she was back." Alan was alert and interested, his attention caught. This Megan Patterson must be someone special, Angie surmised. Although she was curious, she couldn't help feeling an unfamiliar stab of jealousy.

"Champagne and toasts, you say? I guess that means she was successful, then." Observing Angie's piqued expression, he explained succinctly. "Megan's an accountant. A damned good one. Worked in Sydney till she came home because her mother was dying of cancer. Oxley Crossing was hard hit a few years back, when the big banks closed their rural branches. With her experience, Megan headed up a committee aimed at setting up a community bank."

Angie nodded. She'd seen several television documentaries on the topic, and understood what he meant.

"When we'd pledged enough shares to raise the minimum financial stake, she went to talk turkey some more with the principals. Sounds like it's a goer. Wish I'd known she was back. I'd have joined in the celebration."

He caught Angie's incipient frown. "No sweat, though. I'll call her tomorrow. Tonight, is for us, Angie Darlin'. I would much rather make love with you, than discuss money matters with Megan Patterson."

He reached across the table for her hand, planting a hot, moist kiss on her palm and closing her fingers over it.

"She's awfully young to be starting up a bank, isn't she?"

Satisfying as Alan's romantic gesture had been, Angie was still absorbed by Megan Patterson, envying the other woman her achievements and obvious high standing in the community.

"Late twenties; older than she looks," Alan replied, losing interest.

"Besides, it's only going to be a small branch, and she won't have anything to do with running it. Now! Enough about Megan and the bank. If you've eaten your fill, Milady Angelica, perhaps you'll consent to adjourn. Leave the dishes," he added when she began clearing the table, "I'll get them tomorrow."

Ignoring him, Angie continued carrying dishes into the kitchen and loading them into the dishwasher.

"Tomorrow the rubbish will be caked on hard. Do them now, while they'll be easy, then we can have fun with a clear conscience."

~~~~~

Back in her own bed at 'The Victoria' sometime long past midnight, Angie stretched luxuriously with an almost feline contentment.

A considerate and innovative lover, Alan had been all she had expected; hoped for; and then some. Having been lifted to teeter on the peak again and again, the final cataclysm, when it came, raised her to undreamt of heights of ecstasy. Mutual ecstasy, Alan timing his climax to coincide with hers.

And that had only been the beginning. The initial, all-consuming urgency having burnt itself out, they had proceeded to indulge themselves to the fullest; the second and third times being slower, with more time for exploration and experimentation; more finesse; and even more fulfilling in the end.

Half asleep, she trailed one hand down the length of her body; reliving in memory, Alan's intimate caresses.

From breasts, tender and ultra-sensitive following his assiduous ministrations, her hand drifted across the flat plain of her tummy, fingertips brushing the outer edge of the curls hiding the core of her femininity.

Sighing, she recalled how delightfully intrigued he had been to discover the rich colour of those curls, which, flaming dramatically against her milk-white skin, were several shades darker than the bright carroty red hair adorning her head.

Longing to spend the whole night at the cottage, to fall asleep, sheltered in the cradle of her lover's strong arms and wake together in the morning to love each other once again, she had grumbled her displeasure when Alan slapped her lightly on the rump, and ordered her into her clothes.

So much for dreams, she thought, rebellion rousing her to complain. Tersely practical, he had quoted her own pragmatic maxim back at her.

"Practicalities, Angelica. There's nothing I'd like better than to spend every spare moment with you, only it can't be done. I start work at sun-up. You can sleep in as late as you like if I take you home now."

Immediately contrite, she realised she was being selfish. She was free to sleep as late as she liked. Alan, though, would get little enough sleep as it was. *One day, though*, she promised herself. Even farmers were entitled to the occasional day off.

I still have Thursday to look forward to, she remembered. On Thursday, he'd be waiting at the end of her shift, to bring her back to the cottage. On the short drive into town, Alan withdrew into himself, emerging when they rumbled over the wooden deck of the bridge.

"You're important to me, Angie, but I have other commitments too, and some of them must take precedence. Weekends are reserved for my kids. Always." His jaw clenched pugnaciously, as if expecting an argument from her. Receiving none, his tension eased and he continued in a dispassionate tone.

"We'll fit our times together around your work, my work and family responsibilities, and the availability of our love-shack."

He'd let Angie have her own way, so far, but it was time to take a stand, or she'd be trying to rule him in everything. "Mum has been wonderful with the girls, but I don't like to impose too often; so, don't expect to see me more than a couple of times a week."

Angie bit her lip, holding back her instinctive protest at being relegated to the sidelines of Alan's life when she yearned to occupy the centre ground. She understood the constraints on the time they could allot to being private together, yet couldn't Alan see the advantages of including her in some of his family activities as was normal for couples?

Alone in the world, she had long craved a family of her own, and was positive she'd adore his little girls.

"Ah, Angie Darlin'. Don't look so sad." Alan, misreading her sombre expression, wrapped an arm around her. Once parked, he smothered her with kisses, once again her warm, passionate lover.

"I want more too," he whispered. "Much, much more, only it can't be, Angie Darlin'. There's just no way round it."

Give me time, she yawned. *I'll show him there is a way. A simple way; but not tonight when we're both so tired.*

Sated and weary, Alan smiled contentedly to himself on his drive home. Little Angelica Wilson was one hot-blooded, adventurous woman. He considered himself proficient in bed, but she'd taught him a couple of fresh moves, inspiring him to new heights of performance.

Sex with Angie was the best he'd ever experienced, he thought, tomcat smug. He'd never had a lover as generous in giving *him* pleasure. He was more used to women who made it all about themselves. Inevitably, this idyll would come to an end, but hopefully not for quite a long time. He could take a lot more episodes like tonight's.

For a moment, when he was laying down the ground-rules, he'd thought she might kick up a bit of a fuss.

No problem in the end, though, he mused, cynicism turning his mouth down at the corners. *She's no different to any other woman. A few kisses, and some sweet talking, and she's putty.* There shouldn't be too much difficulty keeping his sexy little barmaid in her rightful place.

Her sort knows how to play the game.

Full of confidence, he sang along to the country music station the radio was tuned to.

Over the next few weeks, most of their dates, by necessity, were hurried liaisons squeezed into the tail-end of the day after Angie finished up in the bar. On these occasions, she let Alan make the decisions; invariably a visit to the cottage.

She and Alan were two very physical people, so she wasn't particularly concerned when their few precious hours together seemed to be spent mainly in bed, entirely to their mutual satisfaction. Especially since, on her days off, when they had more time to enjoy themselves, she insisted they include dinner, or a moonlight picnic beside the creek.

This gave her opportunities to try out her newly acquired culinary skills, and she delighted in cooking for Alan, showing off her growing repertoire of dishes. These were the dates she looked forward to, eagerly counting the days till her next break. It had surprised her to discover how much fun cooking was, when you had a good teacher; and Marge was the best.

These happy times, working side by side with Alan in the kitchen, she could almost imagine they were living together, and she glowed with happiness. She'd thought about suggesting they really live together, but felt that might be tempting fate. The two other times she'd moved in with a boyfriend had both ended badly. Besides, they'd only known each other for a very short time.

That decided, Angie put even more effort into getting to know Alan better, a procedure she found unexpectedly difficult.

Every time she introduced personal topics into their conversations, he distracted her, changing the subject without answering.

Not only that, but now the newness of their relationship had worn off, she was noticing other incidents as well.

Each quite minor in itself, they added up to a disturbing volume of painful slights.

When she read in the local paper about the home win scored by the Under Ten soccer team, the winning goal kicked by Melanie Morgan, she wondered why Alan hadn't invited her to watch the game. The soccer fields were just across the road, and, although she hadn't thought to wander across, Alan knew she never worked in the mornings, which was when the youngest children played.

Trying to be fair, she supposed he wasn't used to having a girlfriend to help him cheer for his daughters. She made a mental note to find out the roster and take herself across to the next home game, if he forgot to ask her again.

Even more distressing, was learning from the bar gossip about his parent's anniversary party. It seemed Alan had invited half the population of The Crossing to a barbecue at 'Morgan's Run' last Saturday night. Admittedly, she usually worked Saturday nights, but Phil would have changed the roster if she'd asked.

If Alan had asked.

Her happiness was further dimmed, when she thought back, realising there had been no more lunches or coffees at Tan's when he made a trip into town on farm business. In fact, now she thought about it, they hadn't been anywhere together.

Except to bed.

If Alan Morgan thought he could treat Angie Wilson as if she was just there to serve his sexual convenience, he'd better think again.

On Tuesday, when Alan told her he was taking the day off, and would collect her at ten, she made plans to address the appalling situation.

8

"Why are you getting dressed so early, Angie Darlin'?" Hands clasped loosely behind his head, Alan lay sprawled against the pillows, lazily watching Angie dressing. *Almost as arousing as watching her undress*, he thought.

"Is it so I can have all the fun of undressing you all over again?" His body stirred with renewed interest.

"Not this time, lover boy. Maybe later, if you're good."

"Aren't I always?" He grinned, as she turned an exasperated glare in his direction, disappointed when she failed to rise to the bait.

"Five minutes, Alan. Get your pants on." Scooping his clothes up from where he'd carelessly dropped them on the floor, she leaned over to dump them on top of him. Lunging across the bed, Alan caught her by the wrist. Snaking one long, sinewy arm around her waist, he gathered her onto his lap.

"Gotcha Darlin'." He laughed in triumph. "Now, be a good girl and come back to bed. We've got hours yet before we have to leave."

He had been surprised to hear Angie running the shower, on what he had assumed to be a routine bathroom visit. He was even more surprised now, when she wrenched herself impatiently out of his arms and scuttled across the room; out of his reach, unless he wanted to get up and chase after her.

At the door, she looked back, clearly annoyed.

"Five minutes, Alan Morgan," she repeated, "or I'm going without you. It's far too nice a day to be cooped up inside. And tidy the bed when you get out of it."

There was a distinct snap to her voice, matched by what could only be termed a flounce, as she headed for the kitchen. He supposed she had a point. It was a perfect winter's day, and it would be pleasant outside.

~~~~~

"Oh good. I'm glad you decided to come."

Far from being in a snit as he'd thought, Angie was all smiles. Sliding a freshly brewed thermos of coffee into the holder on her insulated picnic basket, she pushed it towards Alan, "You carry this, Darling, and I'll carry the rug."

With that, she led the way outside, gripping his spare hand and firmly steering him in the opposite direction when he headed automatically for the ute, parked in the shade of the ancient coolabah tree growing on the nearby creekbank.

"Let's walk," she directed. "I thought we could take our lunch down to Rainbow Falls. If we leave the basket in the barbecue shelter, we'll have time to follow the creek up through the gorge, then back around the other side of the hill before it's time to eat."

She wanted to build a catalogue of more shared experiences with Alan than those which could be enjoyed in the bedroom, much as she relished those; and this walking track, conveniently close to the cottage, was one Eddie Turner, the librarian, had introduced her to last week.

They were seated side by side on a rock ledge high above the falls, when she broached the subject occupying her mind. "Darling, Rhonda Molinar and I have become good friends, and she's invited us both to dinner on Thursday night. I've cleared it with Phil, so that's alright. What time shall I tell her we'll be there?" James Molinar, Rhonda's husband, was a long-time friend of Alan's, and Angie was feeling quite excited about sharing a night together, in the company of good friends.

She viewed it as an important step forward in their relationship. A lot of thinking had gone into trying to see them from his point of view, and being charitable, she had concluded his exclusion of her was simply an oversight; since apparently, he hadn't had a proper girlfriend in ages.

Damn! Alan thought. This was just what he didn't need, Rhonda Molinar giving Angie ideas.

Socialising with his friends was not how he chose to spend his time with Angie.

"Thursday? I'm sorry Darlin', but I won't be able to make it,' he said, improvising rapidly.

"I was going to tell you before we left here today. There's a Farmers' Federation meeting I can't get out of." It was true there was a meeting, one he had already talked his father into attending in his stead.

He wondered what the Old Man was going to say when he informed him he'd changed his mind. Something acerbic, Alan was sure, since he hadn't wanted to go in the first place. However, his father's displeasure was preferable to being openly paired off with Angie Wilson, something he'd been taking such pains to avoid.

If he let that happen, next thing he knew the gossips would have them walking down the aisle.

"Alan!" Angie wailed. "Rhonda picked that date especially, because you told me you'd be in to see me."

"At the time, I thought I would be free." Alan was all sympathy. "It's unfortunate my plans were changed. I'll make it up to you next week."

Angie pouted a minute or two, then shrugged. She'd ask Rhonda to reschedule, and next time there weren't going to be any glitches.

"If you can't, you can't," she murmured, earning a kiss for her understanding.

She had intended telling him today about the special project she was working on, but wasn't in the mood anymore. *I'll let it be a surprise for him, too, as well as everyone else,* she decided, hugging her secret to herself. Angie smiled, anticipating Alan's pride when she presented him with the finished product.

It wasn't a new bank, but it was something of value to Oxley Crossing.

Something she had thought of herself, and carried out with only a little help from a couple of her new friends. She felt justifiably proud of herself.

~~~~~

"Time to go, Angie Darlin'." Looking at his watch after they'd consumed the gourmet picnic Angie had packed, Alan sat up on the rug. Tidying up quickly, they ambled back to the cottage, fingers laced together.

Sated with good loving, good food and fresh air, Alan was a happy man, secure in his belief he had the best of both worlds. A wonderful family; work which fulfilled him; and his beautiful, sexy Angie on the side, whenever he felt in need of a little loving.

I must remember to buy her a decent present next time I'm in Tamworth. She's more than earned one, he thought.

"What's the hurry, Darling?" Angie leaned her head against his shoulder, tilting her chin up to see his face.

"I promised to pick the girls up after school. I don't want to be late, or they might get confused about whether or not to catch the bus."

Sudden inspiration struck. This was the perfect opportunity, Angie decided, to give Alan a gentle nudge in the right direction. Even more so in view of her disappointment over Rhonda's dinner party.

"Alan," she exclaimed, beaming with joy, "I've got a great idea. You know, I've been dying to meet Melanie and Jocelyn, so why don't we take them for an icecream. We girls can get acquainted."

Jolted out of his complacency, Alan halted abruptly, forgetting all his usual efforts at diplomacy.

"I don't think that's a good idea at all," he snapped, dropping her hand. "There's no reason what-so-ever for you and my girls to get acquainted."

"Why ever not?" Angie swung round to confront him, her heartbeat racing out of control at his angry reception of her simple suggestion. She essayed a faltering smile, sickened when it met with a black scowl.

"Surely, I don't have to spell it out for you, Angie? Or do I?"

Alan's mouth compressed to a grim, white line, suspicious eyes narrowing to steely glints. He spelt it out, leaving no room for misunderstanding his meaning.

"There's no reason, at all, for my daughters to be introduced to my mistress."

"Mistress? Mistress? Is that how you see me?"

What century is he living in? she wondered, despairing. "Are you calling me a whore?" Angie's voice cracked on the word. "Is *that* what you think I am? A whore?"

Cut to the quick by the terrible, demeaning insult from the man she just this minute realised she loved, her temper, the only thing keeping her upright, raised her now screaming voice several decibels.

"I'm your lover, Alan Morgan. Your girlfriend. Not, I repeat, *not,* your mistress. I am not your 'kept woman'."

Reciprocating anger running wild, Alan yelled back. "Mistress. Lover Whatever. Either way, Angie, you have no place in my kids' lives. Your role is to occupy my bed from time to time."

Her face white, voice shaking, Angie was desperate to salvage her heart from the wreckage.

"I love you, Alan," she whispered, temper dissipating into bleak despair. She could have kicked herself for letting it slip out with such awful timing, but she couldn't take it back. She doggedly ploughed on.

"I believed we were building a proper relationship. I believed we had a future together; that it was what you wanted, too. I believed you were beginning to love me back. How can you demean us both with such archaic claptrap?"

"Love!" Alan sneered. "You mean lust, don't you? You wanted me as badly as I wanted you, Angie, so don't even try to deny it. And don't try to pretty it up by calling it love."

"Yes, I wanted you; and I was honest enough to act on my feelings; but I always felt affection as well. Even that first time, I felt stirrings of love."

I did, she argued silently. *I just didn't recognise it then. All I knew was how happy I was*.

"I thought you were a decent, honourable man; one I could trust. Instead I find you're one of those despicable toads who think barmaid is spelt W_H_O_R_E."

Tears were beginning to trickle silently down her cheeks, and she was holding on to self-control by her fingernails.

"Next thing you'll be telling me you expected me to marry you," Alan scoffed. Peering into Angie's stricken face, he drew a furious breath. "You did, didn't you? You thought I was besotted enough to marry you!"

A thunderous scowl darkening his features, he raged at her, each word a hammer-blow to her heart. "You can forget that little scheme, Angelica Wilson. I don't intend to marry anyone. Once in that trap was enough, but if I did, why would I want to marry you? A woman whose morals are in the gutter?" he jeered.

Wounded beyond endurance, Angie turned jerkily and began running, stumbling dangerously when tears blinded her eyes to the potholes in the gravel track. Behind her Alan swore vociferously, yelling at her to stop. Compelled by an urgent need to outrun her pain, she raced on. Half a kilometre down the track, Alan caught up to her in the ute. Leaning across the seat, he flung open the passenger door.

"Get in, Angie, and stop mucking about," he bellowed, striving to make himself heard above the engine noise.

Deaf to his command, Angie stumbled on. Edging the ute forward, Alan kept pace, anger and frustration colouring his repeated demands that she 'Get in'.

Furious at being ignored, he drove ahead a short distance and stopped. Rounding the front of the cab, he picked her up bodily, and tossed her into the passenger seat; holding her down when she struggled to escape.

"Stop that, Angie! Right now! You're behaving childishly. I'm not going to drive off and leave you, so don't think it." Accepting defeat, Angie buckled her seat-belt and slumped into the corner of her seat; putting as much distance as she could between herself and Alan.

Resuming his own seat, Alan floored the accelerator, gravel spurting from beneath the wheels. Easing back to the speed limit, he glanced impatiently at his passenger, then took a sharper look, his conscience beginning to prick as he observed Angie's stony-faced rigidity, her drying tears tracking dirty streaks down her cheeks.

He had thought she was play-acting to make him feel guilty, only now realising her distress was all too real. Temper cooling, he attempted to make amends.

"Ah, Angie. I'm sorry I was so hard on you." He reached across and laid his hand on her thigh, rubbing gently as he offered comfort. "I thought you understood. I thought a girl like you would appreciate our little arrangement without my having to spell it out. You ought to have known marriage didn't enter into it," Alan cajoled, his voice becoming warm and seductive as he sought to coax her into a more compliant mood.

At the touch of Alan's hand on her thigh, revulsion shuddered through Angie's slender frame. Pushing his hand aside, she sat up straight, contempt in every rigid inch.

"A girl like me, who's been around?" she spat. "Just because I was too honest to pretend about how much I needed you, Alan Morgan, don't you make the mistake of thinking I sleep around. I don't. I'm twenty-three, and you're only the third man I've ever been with, and each of the other times it was for love, too."

Angie gulp back her tears, determined to finish what she had to say.

"The truth is, a barmaid isn't good enough to be seen alongside a Morgan of 'Morgan's Run', is she?" Angie unbuckled the seat belt and stepped down from the cab. Seeing her basket in the back, she snatched it up and started for the front door. Changing her mind, she swung back to give that despicable rat one last, bitter broadside.

"Incidentally, it was you, not me, who brought up the subject of marriage. I was only thinking of myself as your girlfriend. Maybe those old fossils who maintain a girl should save herself for marriage, have the right of it, after all. It's not too late to learn, though, so I reckon the next time a man shares my bed, he better put a ring on my finger first."

Whirling about, Angie, head high, marched up to the door, not deigning to look back.

"Damn!" The curse exploded from Alan's lips. Thumping the steering wheel for extra emphasis, he was about to chase after Angie, when he caught sight of his watch. Indecisive, he looked at the door closing behind Angie, and back at his watch. "Damn!" he swore again, turning the key in the ignition. His girls were waiting.

Angie Wilson would keep.

9

I'm not crying! I won't!

Shock had brought on Angie's earlier paroxysm of grief, and there was no shame in that. To weep beyond the first uncontrolled outburst, wallowing in self-pity, was unacceptable.

Angie Wilson refused to shed tears over her worthless louse of an ex-lover. And ex, Alan Morgan was, as from right now, she lectured herself. No apology could excuse the unforgiveable things he'd said. Lying on her bed with a damp cloth cooling hot, aching eyes, she held the tears back, her teeth gritted so tightly she felt her jaw might break. The whole disastrous confrontation with Alan replayed over and over in her mind, until she forced herself to face up to it.

I did nothing wrong, she concluded. *It wasn't wrong to make love with him. Love is never wrong. Impetuous and foolhardy, undoubtedly, as it turned out. Wrong; no.*

Neither was it wrong to want more. It was Alan who behaved badly; taking everything I gave and yet being ashamed to be seen with me, as if I might contaminate his precious family. Even thinking me such a pathetic specimen of womanhood, he must have known I'd find out the truth, sooner or later. What did he think I would do then? I'm better off without the arrogant, rotten louse.

At this point her self-control wavered alarmingly.

It was one thing to believe all this. Quite another to live with the results. Her treacherous thoughts circled round to the good times they'd shared, and how much she'd grown to love Alan. Then she would remind herself of his cruel words, reinforcing her resolve to expunge him from her life, if not her memory.

It was hard to endure Marge's gentle fussing when she showed herself at dinner, truthfully blaming her washed-out, strained demeanour on a headache. Since her work placed her in the public eye, she had decided the sooner she braved the scrutiny of her friends, and learned to cope with her pain, the better. But enough was enough.

The tablets Marge had pressed upon her in her hand, she stood to leave the dining room. When her phone rang, she checked the caller ID. Seeing it was Alan, she almost succumbed to temptation, at the last minute switching it off without answering.

She'd said all that needed to be said.

She was half-way up the stairs when Marge called her to the phone in Reception.

"It's Alan, dear," Marge whispered. "A nice little chat with your young man will cheer you up, and do your poor head more good than my tablets," she concluded with a conspiratorial wink, handing the phone to Angie.

If only Marge knew.

Angie gave her friend a weak smile, tempted to make an excuse to refuse the call. But, to do so would inevitably lead to long, tedious explanations she wasn't ready to make; although God knew, the last thing she wanted was to go another round with the damned man. Only the dread of him becoming embarrassingly persistent, enabled her to put the phone to her ear, waiting till Marge discretely closed the door before she spoke.

"Angie Wilson speaking." There was grim satisfaction in hearing the normality of her tone, despite her white-knuckled grip on the handset.

"Angie Darlin', it's Alan here." He paused, waiting for her return greeting.

Choking up at the sound of his voice, Angie found articulation impossible, and remained silent. Alan continued, all velvety persuasion.

"I'm so sorry about this afternoon, Darlin'. My wretched temper got the better of me and …"

At that point, Angie's own ready temper flared anew, breaking her vocal impasse. It hadn't been Alan's temper which upset her so badly; it had been his cruel lack of respect for her.

His whole rotten attitude, in fact. Now, it sounded as if he was trying to do a whitewash job. It was utterly intolerable!

"If you're working up to a genuine apology, Alan, fine. I'll listen."

"But Angie, I've already apologised. I'm sorry I lost my temper and upset you."

"That's it? Bullcrap, Alan. Stop wasting my time!" She crunched the phone down with more force than necessary. Almost immediately, it rang again. Sighing, and drawing in a deep, steadying breath, she picked it up before Marge came running to answer, and held it to her ear without bothering to identify herself.

"Angie? Don't hang up again." Alan snapped, seriously annoyed his attempt to resolve their quarrel had elicited such a rude reception.

Angie sighed. It seemed he wasn't going to let up until he'd had his say.

Recovering his composure, Alan realised he needed to be more conciliatory, since his Angie was still upset with him. He reverted to his most persuasive tone. "You're a very special lady, Angie, and there's a really rare and strong connection between us. We'd be foolish to simply throw away everything we could be together because of a silly misunderstanding. We need to talk, Angie Darlin'."

Half-listening, she rehearsed her response. While she agreed with most of what he said, she took exception to the bit about the 'silly misunderstanding'.

"So, what do you say, Darlin'?" Alan had ended up by proposing they take a couple of days to let the dust settle, then get together again as already planned.

Before the bottom fell out of my world. He's acting as if nothing important has occurred. The damned man isn't getting away with treating me as if I'm a half-wit.

Her voice cold and emotionless, belying the nausea roiling in her stomach, Angie stated her case.

"For starters, Alan," she said, "your *abuse* this afternoon went way beyond a mere argument. Secondly, if that rigmarole I just listened to was intended as an apology, it fell far short of the mark. Not one word you said addressed the real issue. We're finished, Alan. Get used to it. And, if you ring again, I'll be forced to explain to Marge why I refuse to speak to you."

This time when she hung up, she didn't linger. She'd had all she could take on what felt like the worst day of her life. She headed straight to bed, swallowing Marge's tablets and pulling the covers up over her ears.

~~~~~

Angie spent the night restlessly tossing and turning; starting up out of hazily recalled nightmares to toss and turn some more. The following nights were little better; but if the nights were taking a sad toll, at least her days were close to normal.

Because Alan had never occupied a prominent role in her public life, she found relief in throwing herself into her daily activities. If she expended more energy than usual in her exercise class, or swam a few extra laps in the pool, no-one noticed except herself. No-one noticed, either, how, at work behind the bar, she chattered more brightly, laughed more gaily, with the customers.

Now she didn't have to save her precious nights off, she had ample time for other activities. Ben Wright, a frequent diner at 'The Victoria', and school principal, had become her friend. Persuaded by his confidence in her, she joined a Tuesday night creative writing group he conducted each week. She wasn't looking to achieve anything special from participating in the group, but it helped to fill her waking hours, and concentrating on writing stopped her from thinking about her loss.

To her surprise, she thoroughly enjoyed herself, and spent several hours over the next few days preparing a short piece to share at the next session.

Alan's ute had been parked outside Pete Hackett's one morning, causing her to instantly change direction, taking a circuitous route home to avoid the possibility of an accidental encounter.

The strength of the temptation to deliberately force just such an 'accidental' meeting appalled her. If she still wanted him so much; loved him, damn it all; perhaps she should give some thought to trying to salvage something from the wreckage?

Always supposing *he* still wanted her, which was not certain.by any means, since, obedient to her command, he'd made himself scarce.

When he strolled into the bar, late Thursday night, sliding onto a stool in front of where she stood, wiping down the counter, her heart leapt, although she was careful not to betray her interest.

When she checked the clock, she doubted he was there for the beer. She'd already begun shutting down for the evening.

"You're too late for anything other than a stubby, Alan." Her manner was pleasant, as if there had never been any bad feeling between them. He was a customer, and she owed it to Phil not to drive paying customers away.

"I'm here for you, Angie Darlin', not the beer." A captivating smile lit up his ruggedly handsome features. Looking beyond the surface, Angie was secretly pleased to note the same signs of sleepless nights she saw in her own mirror.

"I've missed you Angelica Wilson. Don't you think it's time for us to kiss and make up?"

"Let me finish here, then we can talk about it."

Alan nodded, his eyes tracking her movements as she saw the last customers off the premises, cleared tables, and stacked glasses into the dishwasher. All the time she performed her routine tasks, Angie considered her options. If he had come to his senses, was ready to admit to what he'd done, and showed genuine remorse, there was nothing she'd like better than to make up.

Only, this time around, she'd insist on them both putting their cards on the table first. Ready at last, she moved to stand by his side.

"I missed you too, Alan," Angie admitted, barely glancing at him. "Kiss and make up sounds good to me, as long as you really mean it. Give me a minute to fetch a jacket, and we can go outside and talk."

Returning downstairs and shooing him out the door, she took a moment to study his triumphant grin with misgiving.

He was altogether too confident, considering nothing had been decided yet.

Barely giving her time to lock the door behind her, Alan wrapped her in a bearhug embrace, his lips claiming hers with searing passion, rousing her to an answering passion. Breaking apart at last, Alan led her off into the dark car park.

"Let's go, Darlin'. We've got some serious making up to do." He'd learned his lesson; the phone left too much room for Angie to generate resistance. Face to face, she was willing to let him sweep her off her feet. He congratulated himself on his strategy.

He had the door of the ute open before Angie came to her senses.

"Where do you think we're going?" she asked, backpedalling a couple of steps.

"Our special place, of course, Angie Darlin'. Where else?" Surprised by her show of reluctance following straight after their kiss, when she had been every bit as eager as himself, Alan simply stared at her. Voice husky with desire, he began urging her forward again.

"The champagne is on ice, and I've got supper ready and all." He patted the box containing a pair of emerald earrings, waiting in his pocket, but those were for after they'd made up.

Angie was taken aback. What sort of brainless pushover did he think she was?

"Pretty sure of yourself, weren't you?" The fog of hormone-driven desire clearing from her brain, her observation carried a tart sting. Not waiting for a reply, she backed up, arms crossed in front of her chest.

"I'm not going anywhere with you, Alan Morgan. Not until we get ourselves straightened out on one or two issues." Stepping smartly out of his reach, she set off across the road to the secluded park bench where they had talked once before. Slamming the door shut, Alan strode after her.

Both seething, they sat on either end of the bench, each waiting for the other to speak first.

"Your move, Angie," Alan finally muttered. "You might as well get whatever it is off your chest."

"All right, then. I will. Details aside, we broke up, essentially, because neither of us knew what the other expected of us. I believe we should both be completely honest about our needs and expectations, this time. So, up front, Alan; what do you want from me? Sex on demand like before, or are you proposing something different to your last 'little arrangement'?"

"What's your hang-up with sex? Damn-it-all, Angie, I thought you enjoyed it as much as I do? That's the impression I got, anyway. Now you're acting as if I forced you into it."

Why was nothing ever easy with Angie? More to the point, Alan asked himself, why did he keep coming back? Why couldn't he simply cut his losses and take his pleasures elsewhere?

"I do enjoy making love with you. Making love, Alan. Not just having sex. For me, sex is an integral part of a normal relationship. If we are going to be a couple, then we should do lots of things together, as other couples do. Visit our friends, go to parties, spend time with your family. All the things you refused to do with me before."

"But I don't want to share you, Angie Darlin'," Alan protested, trying to wriggle out of the trap he could feel closing in on him. "You're so special, I can't help being greedy about keeping you all to myself. We had a good thing going before, and we can have it again, if you'll just be reasonable. Don't throw it away, Angie," he pleaded.

Angie snorted. Hadn't the man learned a single, solitary thing from their break-up?

"*You* had a good thing going, you mean. I love you Alan Morgan, but unless you're willing to acknowledge publicly that we are a couple, and treat me with the same respect you would show someone like Megan Patterson, it's pointless talking any longer."

"Megan? Why the hell bring her into it? There's nothing whatever between Megan and I. Surely you know that?"

"I'm not saying there is," she explained doggedly, "just that I want as much respect as you would show her, if there was."

Seeing the obstinate set to Angie's expression, he thought back over what she'd said. "Seems to me, you're trying to blackmail me. It's not going to work, Angie. I told you I'm not interested in that kind of relationship. With you or anybody. I won't be blackmailed. You're good in bed, Darlin', but not that good!"

"Then I guess that's it." Angie stood, looking down at Alan. "No blackmail of any kind was intended. I was simply trying to make you understand my needs. You're the big loser here, you know, Alan. You're so blinded by false beliefs, you're throwing away the real thing."

This time it really was the end. Alan hadn't apologised; and neither was he willing to even consider trying it her way.

Her self-respect made it impossible for Angie to accept less.

Thrusting cold hands into her jacket pockets, Angie turned and walked across the road to let herself in via the side door of 'The Victoria Inn'.

10

Another Thursday night, and once again, Alan slid onto a stool in front of the taps, where Angie couldn't possibly avoid him; no matter how much she might wish to. A customer, she was compelled to serve him.

It was three weeks since they had parted; not nearly long enough for time to have healed her wounds, although she was becoming inured to the pain. After seeing nothing at all of him, she had crossed his trail twice this week already.

The first time there had been no warning. On her way home from the pool, she had cut across the sporting fields as usual, and there he'd been, talking to the groundsman, right on her path.

She had been horribly embarrassed, hurrying past with a hurried greeting which she hoped had been taken to include both men.

Reaching the street, she glanced back under the pretext of checking for almost non-existent traffic, before crossing to the hotel. Alan had been standing utterly still, staring after her; such naked yearning in his eyes she had had to force herself not to run back to him. Not to promise him whatever he wanted, if only he'd take her back. It had been a long time before her body had stopped trembling. Before pulse and respiration returned to normal.

The second time had been easier. Forewarned by the ute, Morgana-le-Fey sitting proudly on guard, she had had a few moments grace to steel herself for the encounter. Refusing to turn tail and run away, she had briefly met his eyes, murmured an indistinct greeting, and continued briskly on her way.

And now, here he is, deliberately plonking himself down in front of me.

Angie took a couple of moments to gather her thoughts, then stepped forward to serve him.

"Hello, Alan. What'll it be, then?" she asked, false bravado covering her nervousness.

"A schooner of draught, thanks, Angie." Sober and intense, Alan lacked his accustomed ebullience. Unnervingly, his eyes tracked Angie's every movement as she poured his beer and passed it across to him. Except for polite thanks, he had nothing to say until she returned with his change.

"You made a good job of Marge's brochure, Angie. It's an excellent piece of work. I never knew you could do stuff like that." Mentally, he gave thanks to his mother for providing him with an irreproachable excuse to open a conversation with Angie.

The previous evening, Barbara Morgan had returned from a meeting of the Progress Association, bursting with news.

"What do you think of this?" she'd asked, tossing a glossy brochure advertising Oxley Crossing, and its businesses and attractions, complete with photos and maps, onto the table in front of her husband and son. She let them examine it thoroughly before consenting to answer their questions.

"This is exactly what we've been asking Council for," she said. "They told us they couldn't afford the expensive design work till next year's budget."

"Then where did this come from," Andrew turned the brochure over in his hands. "It looks a professional job to me. Who forked out the cash?"

"That's the interesting bit. Marge brought it along tonight, and gave us all a copy. It was her birthday while we were on holiday, and her pretty, red-haired barmaid gave her a boxful of these for her birthday. The clever girl designed it herself, and paid for the first print run. Phil reckons she got tired of answering the same questions over and over, but he's all cock-a-hoop. So is Marge. Eddie Turner pushed the shire clerk, and since he only had to find money for printing, they'll be officially released next month in time for the beginning of the tourist season."

"Angie Wilson did this?" Alan, a slightly dazed look on his face, questioned.

"Yes, although Marge did say she insists Ben Wright, the school principal, and Eddie both helped her with the research and formatting."

Barbara cast a sly glance towards her son before continuing.

"Apparently, she's doing some sort of TAFE course online, to qualify her for a job in hospitality management, and marketing is part of it. This started out as an assignment she had to do, and she saw how it could be applied to The Crossing." Barbara answered a few more questions from her husband, before she noticed Alan had gone silent.

She and Andrew had been quite concerned about their son, recently. When rumours first began circulating, linking him with Angie Wilson, they had been quietly pleased to see him coming out of his shell, smiling, and whistling about his work for the first time since his marriage had come crashing down around his ears.

They'd made discreet inquiries about the girl, then, satisfied, had left him to tell them about his budding romance in his own time. Unfortunately, while they were away, something had gone wrong.

Lately, he was terse and irritable, snapping everyone's heads off for no good reason. Even Melanie and Jocelyn were complaining about 'Daddy's bad moods'.

It's a risk, Barbara thought, *but one worth taking. He'll be better off getting it out in the open, instead of bottling it up inside him as he is*. Pinning a cheerful smile on her face, she launched her attack.

"You've got a very intelligent young lady in Angie Wilson, son. I'm dying to meet her. Everyone I talk to seems to have nothing but good to say about her. I do wish you'd bring her home with you one day."

Her courage nose-dived, when Alan flinched as if she had struck him, pain etched in every line of his face.

"You're out of date, Mum. We're not an item anymore," he grated.

Andrew came to his wife's rescue, drawing their son's fire down on his own head.

"Pity you broke up with her, Alan," he observed mildly. "Your mother and I were pleased to see you looking so happy again. Sure you didn't make a mistake?"

"You've got it all wrong, Dad. It wasn't me who broke it off. *She* dumped me." Leaping to his feet, Alan shoved his chair back and headed for the door. Hesitating, he looked back at his parents, sitting in appalled silence, stunned by the hornet's nest they had stirred up.

"As for your question, Dad; yes, I think I did make a mistake. A big one." Anguish ripped his heart to shreds as he strode down the hallway to his own wing.

Until then, he had assiduously avoided examining either his conscience or his deeper feelings.

Discovering his parent's approval of Angie, made a mockery of the arguments he had used against letting her play a larger role in his life. He'd been trying to blame her for their break-up, but now his illusions were all swept away, and he was face to face with the truth of his own culpability.

He had lost Angie through his own bloody pig-headedness. Finally, he faced the truth. Without Angie, his life was a barren desert. She had been right all along.

No self-respecting woman would, or should, stand for being placed in such an ignominious position.

He had been a fool to take exception to her expectations. Especially since all Angie had asked for was to be treated with respect; content to leave further developments to time and chance.

He still shied away from the idea of marriage, but at the same time, he needed Angie Wilson with an unbearable yearning he was afraid to give a name to.

All this swept through his mind as he watched Angie pouring his beer, giving him the strength to humble himself before her.

"Why didn't you tell me about the brochure, Angie? You must have been working on it while we were together." She had told him so much about her various interests; conversations he'd been too impatient to listen to properly, but not once had she even hinted at this.

He felt unreasonably hurt at having been excluded from her confidences.

"Was it because Ben Wright was involved?"

Angie looked about for the excuse offered by some necessary task, but none of the other drinkers in the bar needed her. Her mind was darting wildly, all over the place, making it difficult to concentrate, while her heart urged her towards Alan.

She knew better, but it seemed she still loved the despicable rat. She had glossed over their break-up when questioned, putting it down to unspecified, irreconcilable differences, disguising her heartache with a brittle cheerfulness.

If she thought it might help, she was prepared to leave The Crossing, only why should she have to run away from these people who had taken her into their hearts and homes? The genuine praise her project had garnered, had been balm to an ego long deprived of recognition.

Coming to terms with her aborted love affair was a price she was prepared to pay to stay here where she felt such acceptance from everyone else.

Turning, pride stiffening her backbone, she hungrily drank in the sight of the cheeks she had loved to caress; the lips which had kissed her so thoroughly; the large, calloused hands which had stroked her to ecstasy; and knew she wanted him back.

On her terms, though, or no deal.

She caught his haunted expression, recognising the fear lurking at the back of his eyes; and stopped dithering. She would find a way.

"Not telling you had nothing to do with Ben. We've been friends since the first week I arrived in The Crossing, and he asked to share my table in the dining room. He eats here a couple of times a week, and we've become friends. As school principal, he's helped me out, providing a secure computer for me to do online exams for my TAFE course, and he showed me how to set up my computer for that brochure, and printed the prototype on the school machine."

There was a pugnacious tilt to her chin as she defended her friend that warned Alan to tread lightly.

"Ben's a decent man; a good friend. I like him. Sometimes I wish I could feel more for him."

Angie wiped down the already pristine counter, casting a sidelong glance at Alan, catching a tightening of his lips when she spoke so warmly of Ben.

Good. Let him know he's not the only man on my horizon, she thought. *Maybe then, he might value me more highly.*

"Anyway, I had every intention of telling you; and showing you the prototype to see what you thought of my little project, Alan, on the day we had the picnic at Rainbow Falls."

Her words were abrupt, almost disjointed, she was so tense. It made her horribly uncomfortable talking about that awful day. She took a deep breath, then continued, trying not to be inflammatory.

"Only, you know, I got a bit miffed when you made excuses not to go to the Molinar's with me. So, I didn't."

Just then, Mike Patterson signalled that his table was ready for another round. Thankfully, Angie hurried away, taking her time before returning to where Alan waited; by which time, her composure restored, she felt capable of continuing their conversation.

"I hear you're involved with the Tidy Towns projects Eddie Turner is organising," she said, forestalling any further attempt on Alan's part to introduce personal topics. Unsure if the outcome of this conversation would prove to be any better than the last, she was cherishing the tiny window of normality between them.

Discussing the various Tidy Towns projects, he was working on for Eddie, filled the minutes till Alan drained his glass and stood, ready to leave.

"Angie," He said, unwontedly serious, "I know now, you were right in what you said; what you wanted. I apologise unreservedly for being an arrant, disrespectful fool. You were right to dump me for it. Only, we really did have something special going for us, you know. Ours *is* a very rare connection. Too good to throw away because I'm an idiot. Please," he urged, "can we start again, doing it right this time? Will you give me another chance, Angelica?"

It was her intuitive appreciation of the desperation underlying Alan's earnest plea, which Angie responded to.

He's been as unhappy as me, she realised, recalling how she had once been convinced he unwittingly returned her love. *If only ...*, she thought wistfully, then nodded, her decision made.

This time he had addressed the true issue, and surely love was worth at least one more chance. Only this time round, she'd take care not to let her hormones get the better of her common sense.

They set a date for coffee at Tan's, and Alan headed home, lighter at heart than on his arrival. He was going to have to be very, very careful, he reminded himself.

His Angie had been more generous than he had any right to expect, however, he rather thought she might draw the line at yet another chance if he blew this one.

11

Alan knew Angie had claimed Ben was no more than a friend; but it felt every time he went into town to see her, the damned man was there, propping up the bar. The trouble was, Angie had called Ben a decent man, her attitude subtly comparing the two of them. And his guilty conscience did the rest, informing Alan which of them came out the loser.

To make matters even worse, Ben was a man Alan had liked and admired, been proud to call friend, since he had taken up the position of school principal. He'd always thought Ben somewhat dour, but in Angie's company the man was transformed into a quietly sociable, entertaining companion.

Thank God, he rarely stayed long. Tonight was no exception. Just when Alan feared his jealousy was beginning to show, Ben emptied his glass, and pushed back his stool.

"I'm off, Angie," he called. "Damn," he muttered to himself as he stopped after the first few steps.

"Alan, do me a favour, would you mate. I've brought Angie's writing folder back, and left it out in the car. Come on out and get it, will you? I've got a meeting with the P&C, and Angie will want to discuss her story if I fetch it in, and I don't have time."

"Is this for the creative writing group she joined?"

"That's right. I've encouraged everyone to write a short story to enter in a competition the Tamworth newspaper is sponsoring. Angie wanted me to check hers for grammar and punctuation before she sends it off."

Beside the car, folder in hand, Alan was about to return inside, when Ben stopped him.

Alan raised an eyebrow at the hand gripping his arm, and Ben let go.

"I've been wanting a word with you, Alan. Angie is a very special girl. She's had a lot of obstacles in her life, and it's taken grit and determination to overcome them. She has succeeded admirably, and as her friend, I want her happiness."

He paused, gathering the nerve to expose his feelings to another man; even in such a worthy cause.

"I think I fell a little bit in love with her when we first met; something I never thought would happen again for me. Angie brought my heart out of the darkness my life has been since my wife died, before I arrived in The Crossing, and I'll always be grateful to her for that. Because of Angie, I believe there will be someone again, someday."

Ben toed the gravel of the parking lot, then turned blank eyes towards the trees lining the creekbank. It took a palpable effort to face Alan again.

"I was never the one Angie wanted, and I soon realised there was no spark between us. I was pleased, for you and Angie, both, when you seemed to be falling in love."

Alan shuffled uncomfortably, see-sawing between anger and embarrassment. He began to back away.

"Shit, Alan! You think it's easy to talk to you like this?"

Now it was Ben's quickly suppressed anger flashing out.

"Stand still and let me finish, now I've started. Angie doesn't tattle, but I've got eyes and ears, and it was obvious to the most casual observer the two of you ran into trouble. It's your business; yours and Angie's, and I'm not asking questions. Now, it's equally obvious you're both trying to work things out, and I wish you success."

He drew a deep breath, fearful of intruding, but determined to have his say.

"The point I'm trying to make is; I'm feeling jealous vibes from you, Alan, and there's no need for them. There's nothing beyond friendship between the two of us, but Angie is a very loyal friend. Don't be stupid enough to let her friendship for me become a source of dissension between you. Now get back in there, and if she asks, we were talking about Mel's soccer."

Ben climbed into his 4WD and took off, leaving Alan staring after him, mouth agape. He shook his head, and slowly wandered back inside.

Ben Wright was something else, alright. The question was, could he trust him? He rather thought he could. Far from trying to cut him out with Angie, he seemed to be trying to help him win her.

Angie watched Alan slide back onto the same stool he'd occupied previously. He'd been gone a while, and she wondered what he and Ben had been talking about.

He better not have said anything he shouldn't, she thought.

"Got your folder, Ang. Ben said you wrote a story to enter in a competition. Will you let me read it?"

"Did Ben say anything about it?"

"Nah, he's never going to talk about your work behind your back. It just seemed to me, reading your story would be like sharing a special part of you. It might help me get to know you better, Angie. I'd like that. In fact, I'd like to learn everything there is to know about you. This time I want to share my life with you, too."

His cheeks reddened, but he didn't look away. Angie gave a tiny nod.

"Okay, I guess." She took a sheaf of pages held by a paperclip, from the folder, handing them to him. "The rest is just an idea I had for another story."

This time she was the one who blushed, though, for the life of him, Alan couldn't think why.

Picking up a tray and cleaning cloth, Angie went off to clear a couple of vacated tables, leaving Alan to his reading. When she glanced back, he sported a mile-wide grin, which was a positive sign, since her story was an adaptation of an amusing anecdote from her own distant past.

"I loved it, Ang," he said when she circled back to him a while later. "With talent like this, you should be writing novels, or screen plays. I can just imagine this as a short telemovie."

They continued a desultory conversation, periodically being interrupted by Angie's duties, until closing time, when Angie agreed to a stroll along the creek path.

Alan had hoped for more, but she refused to be rushed into resuming their affair, and he supposed he couldn't blame her. He hoped he didn't die of frustration in the meantime.

Which reminded him, of another request he wanted to make of her.

"Saturday is the last home game for junior soccer," he said, "and I was wondering if you'd like to come and cheer the kids on? We could take the girls for lunch at Tan's afterwards, if you'd like? I didn't say anything last week, because they played away, and I'd promised to take the Hackett kids. Pete's wife, Maree, sprained her wrist and couldn't drive. Even borrowing Mum's car, there were no spare seats, or I would have invited you."

"That's alright, Alan. I worked a double shift last Saturday, so I couldn't have gone anyway. But I'll definitely be at the game this week; as long as you're sure you want me there."

Anxiety tinged her voice. She wouldn't go anywhere near his girls unless she was sure of her welcome. Not after the nasty things he'd said in the past.

Alan felt his cheeks burn, glad it was too dark for Angie to see. Gruffly, he reassured her.

"I meant what I said about sharing my life with you, Ang, and the girls are the most important part of my life. I'm not trying to con you. Not this time, and never again."

Angie was so glad Alan was finally willing to meet her in this, she forgave him his earlier offences. threw her arms around his neck, and kissed him. She leaned into him, lips soft and warm, her mobile mouth moving tantalisingly upon his; and sent his libido soaring When he raised his head a considerable time later, to say,

"I don't suppose ...?"

She almost agreed, but tonight wasn't good for her, and it wouldn't hurt him to wait a little longer. Angie still wasn't entirely convinced his reformation was more than skin deep, but she decided to give him the benefit of the doubt. Unless proven otherwise.

"Not tonight, Alan Darling," she glanced up, stroking his cheek with loving fingers, "but I was wondering if you can get away for a picnic next week? We could include a visit to the cottage, if you like?"

Alan liked. He almost tripped over his tongue accepting her invitations. Both her invitations.

~~~~~

Saturday dawned, clear and sunny, and Angie revelled in the rare, late-winter warmth. Wattle and jonquils already bloomed, scenting the air and pleasing the eye; and daffodil spears were showing golden tips.

There would most likely be at least one more nasty, cold snap, but Spring was hinting at its imminent arrival.

However, the extra swing to her steps on her way to the pool for an early swim, owed more to excited anticipation than the season.

Finally, Alan was allowing her to meet his precious daughters.

Of course, she was ready way too early, prowling restlessly back and forth to look out the front windows for the familiar dusty, white ute. Nine o'clock took an eon to arrive, and then she missed seeing Alan drive in and had to rush downstairs when Marge called.

When she came to a halt, unsure how she should greet him in public, he solved the problem, reaching out to pull her into his arms for a long, heady kiss. Putting space between them at last, he held her by the shoulders, studying her intently.

"Looking good, Angelica. There's no doubting which team you're supporting today."

He grinned approval of her black jeans, black and white striped sweat-shirt, and matching beanie and scarf. "You're a Crossing Currawong supporter for sure. The girls take being junior Currawongs very seriously, and will appreciate your effort."

At the ute, he held open the passenger door, and Angie saw the children leaning forward from the back seat. Butterflies flapped madly in her stomach, as she took in the trepidation on their faces.

She wasn't the only one nervous about this long-deferred meeting. She smiled warmly at them both. As the adult, she felt it was up to her to set the children at their ease.

"Girls," Alan said, "meet my girlfriend, Angelica Wilson. Angie, this is Melanie," he ruffled the girl's tawny-blonde hair, causing her to duck her head and swat his hand in mock annoyance, belied by the warmth of her gap-toothed grin.

"And," Alan then reached out to pull the younger child into an awkward, one-armed hug. "This moppet is Jocelyn. Say hello to Angie, girls."

Dutifully they chorused their hellos, and Angie responded, shaking their hands, and greeting them by name. "I read about your winning goal in the paper a while back, Melanie. Mr Wright," - as well as school principal, Ben was the team coach, and had given her thumbnail sketches of both girls – "told me you're one of his stars. He also told me you're a talented artist, Jocelyn. I'm so proud to meet you both."

Shortly, they pulled into the parking area outside the soccer grounds and the girls ran off to join their friends. After a few steps, Melanie turned back. Grabbing Angie's hand, she urged her forward.

"Come and meet the others," she said. "Daddy's the manager of Jocelyn's team, so he'll be busy organising them, then he has to sit on the bench. I'll look after you, Angie, so you won't be all on your own."

Glancing back at Alan, Angie caught his quick nod, and walked off, swinging Melanie's hand as they crossed to where children and parents were milling around, rubbing liniment into calf muscles, and tying bootlaces, while giving last minute encouragement to Jocelyn's teammates, scheduled to play the first game.

True to her word, Melanie stayed close, talking nineteen to the dozen, although Angie quickly realised she knew several of the young mums from the various groups she'd joined in The Crossing, and most of the dads from seeing them in the pub.

When Ben arrived, he joined the group, chatting for a few minutes before rounding up his team and taking them off to begin warming up. Angie moved further downfield to be closer to Jocelyn who was having a lonely time protecting the goal.

Sensing someone come to stand beside her, she glanced around, discovering Andrew Morgan smiling at her.

Phil had introduced her to him several weeks ago, and although the man had been pleasant enough, they had never exchanged more than a few words. She opened her mouth to speak, but he pre-empted her.

"G'day, Angie. Lovely to see you here. The girls are that excited their father has a girlfriend, they nearly drove him mad with their questions. I'm glad to see you and my son are finally getting your act together."

Angie's mouth gaped wider, till she closed it with a snap.

Is that a sign of approval, or is he being sarcastic? She wondered. Getting her mouth in gear, she managed a weak, "Thank you, Mr Morgan," and an even weaker smile.

"Oh, no need to be so formal, girl. Make it Andrew. I'm hoping you will soon be a regular visitor at 'Morgan's Run'." He raised an eyebrow on observing bright colour flooding her cheeks. Angie was too embarrassed to know where to look, so dropped her eyes to stare at the toes of her best winter ankle boots.

"Thanks for the vote of confidence, Andrew, but … I'm not sure how Alan feels about that. We still have a stack of issues to resolve before we talk about further involvement."

And one of those issues, she thought, *is how to reconcile my long-term goals with being Alan Morgan's girlfriend. Not to mention how long our affair is likely to last.*

"Don't mind me, lass. Babs and I have been waiting very impatiently for our boy to bring you home." Angie breathed a sigh of relief, that Alan's parents were willing to give her a fair trial.

"We keep hearing good things about you from our friends," Andrew continued, "but felt it was Alan's prerogative to make the first move in our getting to know you properly. Never thought a son of mine would be so slow with a pretty girl."

They stood in a companionable silence except for cheering Jocelyn for successfully saving a goal, until Andrew took her arm to lead her away.

"Come on. The game's almost over. Let's nip in before the crowd and grab a cup of tea. Barbara's doing a shift on the canteen, so we should be able to get served quickly." They made desultory conversation while making their way to the canteen, stopping to exchange greetings with friends en route.

"Babs! Look who's here. I'm stealing a march on your son. Think you could rustle up some cuppas?"

"Angie! I'm so happy to meet you. I've been wanting to congratulate you on the excellent job you made of our town brochure. Uh-oh. Game's over. We'll be swamped in a minute. I'll just get your teas, and we'll talk some more over lunch."

Angie's lunch at Tan's with the Morgan family was followed up on Tuesday with the day spent at 'Morgan's Run', assisting Barbara in planning her Farmstay Holiday enterprise, using the two empty cottages and the infrequently occupied shearers' quarters.

Applying knowledge gained from her TAFE course, Angie helped Barbara create an internet marketing program, placing the first set of ads aimed at bringing in bookings for the Spring/Summer tourist season. After dinner, Alan fetched the ute to drive her home; including a stop at their usual cottage. She was really going to miss this cottage when Barbara started taking bookings for it.

Should I feel guilty for hoping this cottage won't be needed very often? she wondered. *Wait and see, I suppose*. Using it had been Alan's idea from the first. She would leave it up to him to think of a way round the potential problem; although from her easy acceptance at 'Morgan's Run', she was beginning to get fresh ideas of her own.

Ideas which held great appeal.

Ideas she felt were better kept to herself; in case she was totally wrong about Alan's feelings for her; as she had been before.

By the time Angie began her shift on Friday afternoon, the bush telegraph was buzzing with the news that Megan Patterson had hired a new mechanic for her father's garage.

Mike had been sent off to hospital by ambulance the week before, having collapsed from a mild heart attack while working on Elizabeth Tan's car. It was expected to be several weeks before Doc Rogers would allow him back to work, if at all.

Speculation regarding the future of the garage was rife, although everyone was united in claiming a permanent closure of such an important business would be detrimental to the whole town. Elizabeth herself, an eyewitness to the hiring, brought the story to Marge.

"Ooh, Marge," she enthused, "wait till you see this Jonathon Armitage. Tall, dark and handsome. Rides a big black Harley. He's really very nice, you know. He's down at the garage right now, putting my car back together at last. I heard Megan tell him to come to you for a room, so you'll soon see for yourself."

"Did you hear that, Angie? I'll put him down the other end of the corridor from you; near the men's bathroom. That way you'll both have privacy when there are no visitors. I'll pop up right away and make sure the room is ready for him. We don't want to give him a poor impression of The Crossing. The garage is too important to all of us to risk losing our new mechanic. I know poor Megan has been ever so worried about the difficulty she's been having, finding someone."

As if Marge's rooms are ever not ready, Angie grinned at her friend's unaccustomed fluster. She guessed it wouldn't hurt her to pay the man a bit of extra attention to make him feel welcome.

Which she did, later in the evening when Phil made a point of introducing Jon to her since she'd missed him at dinner.

Marge said he'd been one of the first in the dining room; but when he arrived in the bar, she chatted him up, flirting a little as she did with most of her customers. Not that he hung around for long. In no time at all he was inveigled into playing pool with Joey and his mates.

He asked her out for a ride on his Harley on Saturday afternoon, but, although she liked him, she felt herself totally committed to Alan, so was glad she had to work; that way she gave offence to no-one.

Unfortunately, she also had to work on Sunday, Phil asking her to swap from evening to day shift when the cricket team played home games. This was the first cricket match of the season, and she had been planning to cheer for Alan and his team. She did attend for a short while and saw him open the batting, but Phil needed her on duty.

With the sports grounds designated an alcohol-free zone, many spectators drifted across the street in search of liquid refreshments, staying to cheer from the hotel verandas. Later, when she was collecting glasses outside, she noticed Alan back in the stands, chatting with Jon, and gave the two of them a wave.

MARRYING ALAN MORGAN

12

Angie glared at Alan as she delivered his beer, saving her smiles for Jonathon Armitage, standing next to him at the crowded bar.

She and Alan had had a wonderful day out in Tamworth on Wednesday, then tonight he had arrived unexpectedly, accusing her of carrying on with Jon behind his back.

"Damn it, Angie. The gossip flying around town has you and Armitage spending your free time, maybe even your nights, carrying on together. Depends who's doing the telling."

Alan had been stewing all day after being treated to this bit of salacious gossip passed on by the truck driver hauling a load of 'Morgan's Run' cattle to the saleyards, and he'd been unable to contain himself any longer. He should have known better.

Friday nights were far too busy for Angie to spare him the time to sort something this serious out satisfactorily.

The accusation had spewed out before he had time to guard his tongue, with the entirely predictable result.

Angie was spitting chips, and he was in the doghouse.

Swallowing a gasp, she had turned bright red with supressed anger, emerald sparks flashing from her eyes, glaring into his.

"Outside," she hissed, nodding towards the back corridor. "Phil, back in a minute," she called down the bar, letting her boss know he was on his own. She hustled to catch up with Alan, shoving him roughly through the back door, where she stood, arms akimbo, confronting him.

"Listen good, Alan Morgan. I've only got time to say this once. I am not a cheat. I am not 'carrying on' with anyone except you. For as long as we are together, it will stay that way. Believe me or not, as you like. Now, I'm going back in where Phil needs me."

Without another word, she had pushed past him, returning to the bar. Alan would swear he'd seen steam rising from her ears in the cool night air.

Damn! Damn! Damn! He'd really put his foot in it, he realised.

Did he believe her, though?

He didn't need to think about that at all. It hadn't been the gossip, he realised, which had stirred him up. Over the last few years, he'd had plenty of experience of the gross exaggerations The Crossing's gossipmongers were capable of

It had been the chilling fear he'd lost Angie to a rival, rather than any doubts about her integrity, that led to his loss of control.

By now, he knew his Angie well enough to trust her, but he'd been guilty of treating her very badly, and was unsure how far her forgiveness would stretch.

What if she decided he was too much trouble?

What might happen if, one day, someone else, someone like Ben Wright, or a newcomer like Jonathon Armitage, made her a better offer? Turning and hurrying after her, he tried to explain, but, temper up, she refused to listen.

Knowing it was futile trying to talk seriously on a busy Friday night, Alan wandered over to the park and sat down to think.

Just how important to him was Angie Wilson?

More than when I first fell in lust for her, that's for sure. She'd dumped him once. How would he feel if she did it again, this time for keeps?

Just the thought of it made him feel sick.

So, he asked himself, *what inducement to stay with me can I offer that might be acceptable to her?* The answer to that brought him out in a cold sweat. He had an uncomfortable conviction that for a long-term affair, and he squirmed, realising how very, very long term he wanted their affair to last, he'd have to go the max.

He hadn't planned to marry again, but if that was what it took to keep Angie …?

Could he do it?

Did he want her that badly?

More to the point, would she believe he meant it?

Despite Angie's pragmatic approach to life and love, he'd more than once felt she was denying a softer, more romantic side to her nature, which she wasn't aware of herself.

If he didn't mean what he said, and she called him on it, he knew he'd be sunk.

Tonight was make or break for him. Let Angie go; or be prepared to sign on for the long haul.

It was a good half hour before he reappeared in the bar, grim and determined, to discover the first test of his resolution. Jonathon Armitage was propping up the bar on Phil's end, chatting desultorily with Pete Hackett.

Alan glanced in the other direction, catching Angie watching him, a scowl darkening her face. Taking a deep breath, he nodded to her, giving her a tight smile, and set out to demonstrate his belief in her by being friendly towards his rival.

He joined Pete and Jon, and, when Pete left, invited the other man to join him in the pool room.

He had to grit his teeth and bear it when his Angie demonstrated her disdain, flirting outrageously with Jon while practically ignoring himself. If Jon's response had been more than perfunctory, he was certain he would have knocked the man's teeth down his damned throat.

It was a long night, waiting impatiently until closing time.

Angie felt nausea curdling her stomach, making her even angrier. How dared Alan Morgan give the slightest credence to that appalling rubbish? If she knew who had started the rumour she'd skin them alive.

Neither she nor Jon had done anything to deserve one iota of blame; and Alan should know without asking, that he could trust her.

She sent another dark scowl in his direction. Why didn't he just go home, out of her sight, so she could relax?

Finally!

"Morgan, bar's closing. Time to go," Phil called to the last customer left hunched miserably over the table in the back corner. He'd bought his last drink more than an hour earlier, making it last, and now Alan pushed himself wearily to his feet.

"Yeah. Okay, Phil. I've just been waiting to have a word with Angie when she's not too busy."

"Up to her, mate. Angie, you're off, Luv. Put this sorry bugger out of his misery. I'll finish up."

"Please Angie," Alan begged, half afraid she might still refuse to talk to him.

Angie put the last glass into the dishwasher and set the machine running. With a yawn, she called 'Goodnight' to Phil, and beckoned Alan to follow her out, leading him across the street to what was now a very familiar park bench.

Alan eyed the inoffensive piece of outdoor furniture askance. "Not sure I like this spot too much," he muttered. "I always seem to leave here completely frustrated."

"If you mean what I think you do, I'll tell up front, Alan; you will be leaving frustrated tonight. I'm utterly exhausted. I only came outside with you because I have something to say that can't wait."

Although it seemed it could wait, for a short time at least, while Angie wiped the dew from the seat before sitting down, turned towards Alan so she could see his face when they talked.

"I've been behaving badly tonight, Alan," she began, surprising him into staring at her, mouth agape. "Even though it's all your fault I was so angry, there was no need for me to drag poor Jon into our disagreement. You don't really believe I'd do what the gossips are saying, do you?"

Tears pooled in the corners of her eyes, although she refused to allow them to fall. She turned her face aside until she had her emotions under control again; missing the pain which flashed into Alan's face, then was gone in the same instant, replaced by a tenderness she hadn't expected.

"God, Angie. I'm so sorry. I trusted you. I really did. Do. It was fear that all my idiotic denial of my feelings for you might cause you to give up on me one day, and turn to someone else, though not necessarily Jon Armitage. I was so tied up in knots, my words came out all wrong, making you think I believed the nonsense I'd heard this morning. I tried to tell you, but you were too quick off the mark, scooting back inside before I had time to speak. Can you possibly forgive me, Darling?"

"I already have."

Alan's surprise was balm to the pain Angie had been suffering tonight, but she couldn't let him off so easily, adding a straight-faced rider which caused the heat to rise in Alan's cheeks.

"You need to stop being an idiot, though, because I don't know how many more times I can forgive you."

During the evening, as she carried out her duties, she had been considering just that point. Then she recalled the discussion on romantic love the first time she'd attended the Creative Writing group.

Eddie Turner had claimed love alone wasn't sufficient basis for a successful marriage, and any writer who offered that scenario was undervaluing their characters. According to Eddie *'You should think of marriage as building a home for the heart. Qualities such as respect, honesty, tolerance, mutual support, trust and all the rest are the bricks, with love the mortar cementing them together.'*

Once again, Angie turned the concept over in her mind, liking it more and more.

Marriage might be a distant, hazy dream on her personal horizon, an outcome which might never eventuate; but she felt sure that to give it a reasonable chance of happening, she needed to start assembling those bricks, and mortaring them together with the love she felt for her stubborn man, whose self-proclaimed idiocy demanded all the tolerance and understanding she could muster.

Beginning immediately.

She took both his hands into her own, and, holding his gaze, spoke from her heart.

"I love you Alan. I don't know where that love will take me. I don't know what you feel for me. You were right though, when you talked about the mutual attraction between us as being too special to throw away. I'm willing to put tonight's argument behind us, if you are, and carry on from here."

"Me too." Alan's reply was muffled as his lips came down on hers, his hands hauling her up against his body. Some considerable time later, when they came up for air, he held her face between gentle work-roughened palms saying,

"This is uncharted territory for me, Angelica, but I'm thinking I love you too. Will you give me time to explore it; get used to the idea?"

"All the time you need, my Darling."

The sweet, tender kiss that followed was all about sealing a pact, and very little at all about the raw sexual need their kisses usually aroused.

And it seemed Angie wasn't as tired as she had previously claimed. And Alan, glancing back over his shoulder, having been granted a practical lesson in the power of words; the right words, that is; felt a surge of affection for his now favourite park bench.

13

"Your bloke's here again. Seems every time I turn around, I'm tripping over him."

Angie, hot-cheeked at what felt like a rebuke from her boss, opened her mouth to apologise, when Phil winked, indicating his grumble was directed towards his audience; and, right on cue, Marge, her matchmaking instincts to the fore, rushed to the defence of the young lovers.

"Don't you listen to him, Angie, love. I reckon if there was more love, the world would be a better place. Your Alan is welcome here as often as he likes. He's in the back lounge with a coffee, waiting for you, Dear."

Her kindness brought the colour flaming in Angie's cheeks all over again. It was Wednesday, not a day Alan was normally free, and she had seen him every day since Saturday night when he'd told her he loved her.

"I'll just get a coffee for myself, then, and see what he wants," she muttered, escaping to the kitchen, leaving Marge and Phil to continue their good-natured wrangling.

~~~~~

"Alan. How lovely to see you again so soon after we talked yesterday."

That didn't come out quite as she'd meant it too, Angie thought, but Phil was right. Alan was using every conceivable excuse to come into town, even if there was only time for a quick kiss and a whispered 'I love you'.

Not that she had any intention of discouraging him; she couldn't hear those three little words often enough.

Far from discouraging him now, she put her coffee down beside his empty mug, and slipped onto his lap to show him how very pleased she was to see him.

"I've got good news, Darling," she whispered. "Jodie Maxwell who works when I'm off, wants to swap shifts, so I'm free on Sunday this week, instead of tonight, which means I can join in with your Tidy Towns project at Rainbow Falls. I'm really looking forward to contributing my bit alongside everyone else who's been volunteering."

"It's no cake-walk, you know," he warned. "We'll be starting early to get it finished in one day."

Angie nodded happily. She wasn't afraid of getting her hands dirty.

The only reason she hadn't joined in before, was that the Sunday afternoon working bees clashed with her duty at the hotel.

Alan grinned, not altogether convinced, but happy to have her join in.

"Okay then. Eddie Turner's out to win this year, so it better be as near perfect as possible. Shall I save you a paint brush, or would you prefer a hammer?" When Angie opted for the paintbrush, he continued.

"After we finish, there should be time for a swim under the falls, then it's back to the homestead for a BBQ. I'm glad you can make it, too, Angie Darlin'. Shall I come in and fetch you?"

"No need. Bob Whitman is taking all of us. I'll meet you there."

After a suitable interval to say goodbye, Alan set Angie back on her feet, picked his Akubra up off the floor beside his chair, and headed for the door. "See you tomorrow night?"

"Absolutely. Bye, Darling."

∾∾∾∾∾

"I love you, Angie Darlin'." Every time he said those words to her, Alan found them easier to say.

And every time Angie rewarded him for saying them, he felt surer of the decision he'd arrived at almost a week before. Last night, instead of packing up and heading for home after making love, they had stayed the night at the cottage, falling asleep in each other's arms, to wake this morning and make love again.

He wondered how it was possible, but he'd swear, that since he'd admitted his feelings to Angie, the loving was better than ever.

Maybe love did make a difference. If so, he was all for it.

"Love you too," Angie murmured back, brushing coppery curls out of her eyes.

"What is it?" she asked, noting the intense way Alan was staring at her. "Have I come out in spots, or something?"

"Or something. Darling, how is it you look prettier every time I see you?" Alan's compliment elicited another long, satisfying kiss. Alan was the first to pull back.

Sitting up, he leaned against the headboard and pulled Angie onto his lap, all with the most serious expression on his face. An expression that made Angie feel inexplicably nervous.

"Angelica Wilson, I love you so much, I want to go on making love with you for the rest of my life. How about it, Darling? Will you marry me?"

His question, quite literally, took Angie's breath away. Nodding enthusiastically, she threw her arms around his neck, finally finding enough of her voice to gasp,

"Yes! Yes! Oh Alan, do you really mean it?"

Joy overwhelmed her, causing her lovely emerald eyes to overflow.

She had been dreaming of marriage for a while, now; but after his earlier assertions on the subject, she'd never imagined Alan shared her dream. He'd succeeded in taking her by surprise, in the most wonderful way.

It wasn't till they were on their way back to town, that Angie came down from the clouds and began talking about wedding plans.

"The first thing we need to do, is set the date," she said, snuggling against Alan's shoulder. "After that, everything else will fall into place."

"How long do you think you'll need to organise the wedding? You know, the dresses, catering, invitations etcetera? I know Mum will get a kick out of helping you, and the girls will be clamouring to be flower girls. Will six months be long enough? We could plan on sometime round April or May, or a little later, even, if you need more time."

"Six months!"

Angie laughed. Surely it wouldn't take as long as that!

"I don't want the fuss of a big traditional event. You know, Alan, for me, the marriage itself is far more important than the celebration. I don't have any family of my own, and apart from a handful of people, most of the friends I'd want to invite are here in The Crossing."

She felt a moment's regret, wishing she could invite her mother, but she had died several years ago, their differences still causing an unbridgeable abyss between them. She shook off the unfamiliar melancholy and continued speaking.

"I reckon an informal garden wedding could be put together very quickly. Let's say one month, maybe a week or two longer if that date doesn't suit either the celebrant or the caterer. Then we'd be married before Christmas."

She sighed voluptuously. "Just think, Darling. Our first Christmas together. You know, I don't think I've ever had a traditional family Christmas. My mother wasn't much for family stuff."

One month! It, wasn't possible. Alan paled beneath his tan.

"Sounds wonderful."

He tried to sound enthusiastic, not sure if he succeeded.

"Unfortunately, I don't think it can be done. Let's compromise," he drawled, hiding his panic. Why hadn't he kept his mouth shut a while longer?

I got carried away by my emotions, that's why.

Now he had to pay the price.

"Christmas is way too soon. Let's say Easter," he suggested as a counter offer.

"But Alan, Easter will be late next year. That would take us back to your original estimate of six months or more. All the flowers will be finished, and a garden wedding wouldn't work. Besides, it'll be cold then, and doesn't it rain in Autumn?" Angie pouted.

Why did Alan have to pick this moment to be difficult?

"Look, we haven't got time to talk this through now." Alan needed more time. He scrambled to think up a good reason to delay the wedding.

"I have to get home and help Dad. We've got a busy schedule today. Tomorrow's Saturday. Why don't I pick you up first thing in the morning and we'll go to Tamworth and find you a nice engagement ring, and we'll look at possible dates."

Alan was right. If setting a date was going to require a lengthy discussion, they'd have to defer it till Saturday. Although why he was so against getting married before Christmas, she simply didn't understand. It was only the end of September. Stacks of time before Christmas.

Either the man wanted to marry her or he didn't.

The disagreement, small though it was, took the shine off Angie's joy.

~~~~~

"Not those." Alan steered Angie away from the display of diamond engagement rings. "Diamonds are okay, Darling, but I think one of these emeralds will suit you better. They match your eyes, and they'll go with all the colours you like, won't they? Tell me what you think?"

"You're so right, sir." The woman assisting them at the jeweller's supported Alan. "Emeralds will enhance your fiancée's vibrant colouring. I'll show you our selection, Angela, and you'll see what I mean."

"Angelica," said Alan. "Angelica, not Angela."

Angie giggled, half from the woman's understandable mistake with her name, and half from nervousness; although why choosing a ring should bring on a bad case of nerves, she didn't know.

She brushed aside the poor woman's stammering apology.

"That's alright. Most people make the same assumption." Her eyes snagged on a lovely, square-cut emerald, flanked by smaller diamonds, set in white gold.

At the same moment, the ring caught Alan's eye, and he picked it up. Reaching for Angie's hand, he slid it onto her finger.

"A perfect fit," he whispered. "Maybe that's prophetic."

Tears sparkled in Angie's eyes, mirroring the green and white fire of the ring as she held her hand out in front of her, admiring the look of it on her finger.

"Yes," she breathed, her voice catching. "I don't need to look any further, Alan Darling. This is the one."

"Looks like you've made a sale in record time," Alan grinned at the saleswoman. "We'll take it, if you're sure you don't need to look at any others, Angie Darlin'."

She nodded, quite sure.

"Leave it where it is. I like seeing my ring on your finger. Now all those other blokes will know you're spoken for."

He chuckled, dodging Angie's playful swat on the shoulder. He was rather pleased with himself. A task he'd feared would take all morning and entail a visit to every jewellery store in Tamworth, was completed to his Angie's satisfaction in less than half an hour.

They filled in the time till lunch wandering round the shops. To Alan's consternation, Angie continued her split-second decision making, resulting in his carting around bags filled with stationery, serviettes, tablecloths and ribbons to be used in decorating tables and chairs.

She had even found a pair of shoes she insisted were absolutely perfect for the gown she had in mind.

It seemed his woman had a very good idea, not only of the length of the guest-list, but exactly everything else she wanted. He began to feel distinctly uncomfortable.

At this rate, Angie would have the whole wedding organised before he had time to reign in her enthusiasm. Not that he didn't want to marry her. He did. Unfortunately, her ideas on the timing were just plain impossible.

When she brought out her diary while they waited for their lunch to be served, and started circling dates, all in November and December, he noted, he forced himself to be firm.

"No, Angie Darlin'. That's the busy time on the farm. I won't be able to get away at such short notice, and you want a nice honeymoon, don't you? Autumn will fit in so much better all round."

Much to his surprise, she stopped arguing for her preferred dates, quietly agreed that he was probably right, put her diary back in her handbag, and sat, eyes cast down, twisting her ring round and round on her finger, to look up and smile at the waitress a few moments later when she arrived with their meals.

Not once, during lunch or on the drive back to The Crossing, did Angie mention anything at all to do with their engagement or wedding, chatting on about a dozen other items of interest to Alan, encouraging him to talk about them at length. So why, having got his own way, did he feel an unbearable tension rising within him?

Outside 'The Victoria', Angie, gathering her precious purchases from the back seat, reached for the door handle.

"Wait up, Angie."

"What is it Alan? I'm on duty in a few minutes. I don't have time to talk now."

"I'll be quick, Darling. I just want to thank you for being so understanding about the dates. I know you're a bit upset about it, but with more time to plan everything, it will all work out better in the long run. You'll see."

He got out and hurried round to help her out with the packages, pulling her to him for a kiss before stepping back so she could go inside.

To his surprise, she dropped the bags on the ground. Fishing around in her handbag, she pulled out the ring box the saleswoman had given her, slipped her engagement ring off, and put it into its box. She looked down at it for a moment, then snapped the lid shut.

She was blinking back tears, her voice wobbly as she handed it to Alan.

"Here Darling. You hold onto this for me. You should have said you needed more time to make a commitment to marrying me. I would have understood, you know. Marriage is too serious not to be absolutely certain. If ...," She gulped back incipient tears, and tried again. "If ..., when you decide you're ready, you can offer it to me again."

By the time she finished tears were trickling down her cheeks, despite her best efforts to suppress them.

She hurriedly turned aside and reclaimed her discarded bags, leaving Alan gaping after her.

"Angie! Don't do this. I do want to marry you. I love you." He reached out to stop her, but she dodged away from his hand, hurrying for the door.

"I am committed to marrying you," he muttered to the empty space Angie had occupied seconds before.

Damn! Damn! Damn!

Why did she always have to come out with stuff like this when there was no time for him to convince her she was wrong?

Alan followed her inside, waiting at the foot of the stairs till she finished changing and came down to take over from Phil in the bar. By then Angie had herself well in hand and wasn't listening to a word he said.

Unable to convince her otherwise, he made his way home, where he took out his frustration splitting firewood and stacking it alongside the shed.

MARRYING ALAN MORGAN

14

Returning that beautiful ring; the symbol of her heart's desire, had cost Angie dearly, but she'd do it again, faced with the same circumstances.

If Alan was so unsure of his commitment that he wanted to defer their wedding indefinitely, then they shouldn't be getting engaged at all.

In her mind, the gap between announcing an engagement, acquiring a marriage licence, and then getting married, was only meant to allow time to make all the necessary arrangements; and, quite sure of her own commitment, the one month mandated by Australian law, was all the time she needed.

She truly believed Alan's spurious arguments spelled uncertainty on his part. She had told him she loved him too much to hold him to a reluctant promise, and even though he'd protested, she hadn't quite believed him. So she still insisted on giving him back his ring.

Now, she didn't know where they stood.

She didn't know if they were still a couple, or whether Alan had washed his hands of her.

She wished she hadn't promised to help on this final stage of the Tidy Towns program, but, her word given, she'd felt honour bound to turn up.

On the drive to Rainbow Falls the next morning, she had covered up her misery with bright chatter, but when Alan Morgan pushing his girls on the swings was the first sight which met her eyes when she stepped down from the back seat of Bob Whitman's 4WD, her courage momentarily failed her.

She hadn't expected him to bring Melanie and Jocelyn on the Sunday working bee. Although she loved the girls, she was afraid that the way she was feeling today, after giving Alan back his ring, their presence might lead to a certain degree of awkwardness.

The girls came running, followed more slowly by their father, and in the melee of greetings, no-one else noticed that Alan hadn't had a word to say to her.

In self defence against Alan's anger, Angie hooked her arm through Jon's, monopolising his attention while they sorted out the various tasks and collected their tools. Paint brush in hand, she made a determined show of concentrating on achieving a neat finish, leaving the desultory chatter to the others.

She didn't think it was her imagination that the discord between herself and Alan had spilled over, affecting Jon Armitage and Megan Patterson as well. They had both been rather terse when accepting their assignments.

Even the girls made themselves scarce, running off to build a dam in the shallows, intent on some complicated game of their own devising.

Her heart so painfully constricted at Alan's continued avoidance of her company, Angie felt incapable of her usual small-talk, even though the tension had eased somewhat by the time they sat round the picnic table for lunch.

Melanie and Jocelyn, swapping places with Bob to sit either side of Jon, had so much to say, comparing their Pee-wee motorbikes with his Harley, that no-one else felt constrained to make conversation. The food disposed of, they were soon hard at work again.

The project completed in record time, they changed into swimmers and went charging into the water. Angie, the last to get changed, the only exception. When Melanie and Jocelyn saw her drop her towel on the grass and walk into the water, they abandoned Jon, and came to join her.

It was safer, and fun besides, to help the girls learn to swim properly, than to splash about on the fringes of the adult group, trying not to let Alan's attitude reduce her to tears. And, she reminded herself, there was the BBQ at 'Morgan's Run' to get through before she could afford to relax her guard.

In the end, the BBQ was surprisingly easy. She and Megan had taken turns showering and changing into the fresh clothes they'd brought with them, then they joined Barbara Morgan cutting up salads, and setting out the food, while Alan took charge of the meat, ably supervised by the other men. Seated round the large, square outdoor table, Angie found herself next to Bob, who was seldom at a loss for words.

The man had political aspirations, and if the ability to pontificate on any and every topic was an essential prerequisite, then he was a shoe-in at the next election. All he needed to keep him talking was a judicious question or two, which Angie willingly supplied as needed.

Pinning a look of keen interest on her face, she sat back and sipped her Tyrell's red, letting everything flow by her. It was something of a shock to hear herself being addressed.

"How's your TAFE course going, Angie?"

"Oh." She dragged herself back into the general conversation. "It's going really well, Megan. Two assignments due this month, then a final exam in November and I'm finished."

"Do you have any plans for the future? Edith Turner mentioned you might be looking for a management position when you're finished."

"That's right. My original plan was to complete the course, then look for a job in the hospitality industry. Unfortunately, that would mean leaving The Crossing, and I really like it here. I feel I've found a place I could be happy for the rest of my life. That's why I'm seriously considering Ben's proposal."

"Ben's proposal? But, ..." Barbara chimed in, glancing uncertainly at her son, whose sudden plunge from happiness to surliness hadn't escaped her notice. She swallowed the impulsive words trembling on the tip of her tongue.

"I hadn't realised you and Ben were seeing each other," she substituted weakly.

Angie was so shocked she almost spilt her wine.

"We're not, Barbara. I didn't mean *that* kind of proposal."

She'd forgotten that no-one knew what she and Ben had been discussing recently. Now the cat was well and truly fighting its way out of the bag.

She put her glass down carefully, and took a steadying breath, in case her aspirations met with scorn.

"I joined the writing group Ben mentors, and he reckons I've got a novel in me. He's suggested I defer my other career options and concentrate on my writing. If I do that, staying on at 'The Victoria' will suit me perfectly. My job there allows me plenty of time to write during the day, when it's quiet."

Angie's words fell into a pool of silence, which, embarrassed, she raced to fill.

"I know. It's a silly idea. As if I could ever hope to succeed at something like that." Nervous, she giggled, eyes fixed on the hands she was wringing in her lap.

"No, Angie. It's not silly at all. If we never tried new things, we'd never discover what we're really capable of."

To Angie's surprise, it was Megan Patterson who came to her defence.

"The fact that Ben Wright thinks you've got what it takes, says a lot, you know, Angie. He doesn't hand out unearned praise. Besides, didn't I hear on the grapevine that you entered a writing comp?"

Angie nodded. "We haven't heard the results, yet."

"Edith Turner was quite impressed with your entry. I say, go for it, Girl. We're all behind you, one hundred percent," added Andrew Morgan.

Everyone else found their voices at the same time, adding further encouragement, talking over the top of each other, wanting to know what her novel was going to be about.

Peeping surreptitiously towards Alan, Angie caught him watching her, unmistakable pride glowing in his eyes. He winked, and gave her one of his slow smiles, and her nerves fled.

Laughing, relieved, she was suddenly, enjoying herself, where previously the party had been such an ordeal.

"Crime, with a smattering of romance thrown in. And that's all I'm telling you. Let me write it first, before you ask any more questions."

Happy though she was to be assured of their support, her writing was still too close to her heart for Angie to be comfortable with the attention. Standing up, she began collecting the empty plates and glasses.

"Let's help Barbara with this lot, shall we?"

"That's okay. The rest of you stay here and have another drink. I'll give Angie a hand."

Alan was quick to pick up the stack of plates, heading for the kitchen with Angie carrying a tray of glasses and salad bowls, right behind him. They made short work of cleaning up, then Alan turned to Angie.

Quiet, and very serious, he told her they needed to talk, and led her onto the back veranda, shutting the door to ensure privacy.

"I love you, Angie. I really do, but you gave me a bad moment just now, with that misunderstanding over Ben. Are we still a couple, or did giving me back your ring mean you're finished with me?"

"Ohh. I thought it was all about you being finished with me. You never spoke to me all day, and you avoided me." There was a sob, hastily swallowed, causing a wobble in Angie's voice.

"I didn't know what to say. You wouldn't listen to me last night. Just because we can't agree on a wedding date doesn't mean I'm not completely committed to you, Angie, because I am. I love you. I want to spend the rest of my life with you."

His words erased the pain from her heart.

Mostly.

She still felt he was prevaricating; unconsciously perhaps, she conceded; otherwise, why the disagreement?

"And I love you, Alan. I have absolutely no doubts, and I hope we'll always be a couple."

The next little while was taken up with mutual expressions of their love. If the distant sound of voices hadn't reminded Alan of their guests, he'd have whisked Angie off to his bedroom and locked the door.

It wasn't till they had rejoined the others, he realised he'd missed his chance. In more ways than one.

Megan was ready to leave, chivvying Bob and Jon towards the car. In the slight scuffle over who should drive, Angie slipped into the front seat beside Megan, waving goodbye to the Morgan family as a whole.

They still hadn't settled their dispute over the date; the ring was still in his bedside drawer; and if he'd been quicker, maybe he could have inveigled Angie into spending the night at the cottage.

He needed to get his act together, that was for sure.

On the plus side, he and his difficult love were speaking again; and he could stop feeling that niggling worry about Jonathon Armitage cutting in on him.

During the swim that afternoon, he'd got the man's attention by thoroughly ducking him, then making it totally clear Angie Wilson belonged to him. Even though, at the time, he hadn't been entirely sure of that himself.

Also, he was taking her to the Literary Awards dinner on Wednesday, to hear the announcement of the competition winners, and they planned to stay in Tamworth overnight.

Life was looking good once again.

15

"G'day, Morgan. Mind if I join you?"

Without waiting for Alan's affirmative grunt, Ben Wright pulled out a chair and sat opposite him at the table in the back of the bar. Thursday evenings were usually quiet, and this one was no exception. He knew there'd be no flapping ears listening to what he intended to be a very private conversation.

He hadn't seen Alan in the two weeks since they'd sat next to each other, cheering when Angie won the Reader's Choice, and Edith was awarded a Highly Commended for their respective short stories

Tonight he'd deliberately sought him out.

"What's wrong with you, Morgan?"

Ben opened the encounter with a full broadside, ignoring his quarry's startled puzzlement.

"I can't trust you to get anything right, can I? Angie's being very tight-lipped, but I'm an observant bugger, and two weeks ago, you and Angie were love's young dream; billing and cooing as if you were the only two people in the world who'd ever been in love. Now, she's got dark circles under her eyes as if she's not sleeping well, and you're sitting here looking the picture of misery. Sit down!" he snapped, as Alan, temper flushing his lean cheeks, made to stand.

Moderating his tone, Ben added, "I care too much to sit back and watch you ruin Angie's life. Or your own."

Alan shrugged, resuming his seat.

"Don't see there's much anyone can do. I thought everything was going great between us, too. If Angie's unhappy, it's because she's just too stubborn to listen to reason."

Even though he'd responded angrily to his friend's interference, he'd been steadily losing ground with Angie, and part of him welcomed a potential ally.

"No details, mate, but problem solving is part of my job description. Very briefly, what's gone wrong?"

He sure wouldn't be sharing any details, Alan thought, suppressing a shudder. Even his parents weren't privy to the truth. He didn't hold out a whole lot of hope, but he understood Ben saw himself in the light of an older brother to Angie.

If anyone could get her to see reason, maybe Ben was the one. All the same, Alan took his time, working out what to say. He was hanging in there, but if something didn't change soon, he was afraid Angie would cut her losses and dump him.

Desperation urged him to take a chance.

"Basically, what happened is, Angie jumped to an incorrect conclusion and refused to listen when I told her she was wrong. It's eating away at her, undermining our relationship."

He took a gulp of his beer, watching with forlorn hope as Ben sat lost in thought, until, glass empty, he signalled Phil to bring another round. The fresh drinks in front of them both, he spoke at last.

"Do you *know* she's wrong, or merely have a gut feeling she's wrong?"

"Know."

Ben nodded. Half his beer disappeared before he continued. "So, Morgan, tell me if I've got this straight. From the available data, Angie formed a conclusion which you, possessing more data than she does, know is incorrect." Alan nodded assent. "What would happen if you shared the missing data with her?"

"She'd kill me." The words spilled out before Alan could stop them.

Ben drained his glass and pushed himself to his feet. A smirk on his face, he clapped Alan on the shoulder.

"Never took you for a coward, Morgan."

Alan glared at his retreating back. If that was Ben's idea of help, it would be the last time he turned to *him*! Even so, the suggestion that he should come clean with Angie had taken root.

The worst she could do was dump him sooner rather than later.

The best …? He'd made so many mistakes, he hardly dared hope.

~~~~~

"You're awfully quiet, Darling."

Angie had finished work, and they were on their way to the cottage. Alan's grim silence was scaring her. Over the last couple of weeks, she had carefully not nagged about the aborted wedding plans; turning the conversation in other directions if Alan appeared to be edging it into dangerous territory.

However, avoidance of the subject had taken its toll on her emotions. Just lately, she had swung from doubting the strength of Alan's love, to suspecting his declared love was no more than his way of keeping her sweet so she'd give him what he wanted. The mere thought of such duplicity made her sick to her stomach.

It was times like this she longed for a mother she could rely on for advice, or failing that, a best friend. It was a pity Megan Patterson hadn't taken her up on her offer of friendship. She admired Megan, and had the instinctive feeling the other woman could be the friend she'd been longing for.

She shrugged off her bout of introspection. There was no point moaning about what couldn't be helped. She turned her attention back to Alan.

"There's something I have to tell you, and I'd rather do it at the cottage."

Where I won't be distracted by driving; and where I'll be able to see how you take it, he could have added.

He hadn't been joking when he'd said she would kill him. His knuckles whitened on the steering wheel.

"O-kay." Angie's hands clasped each other on her lap so tightly they ached. The rest of the short drive seemed interminable.

Finally arrived, Angie dropped her bag on the floor just inside the door. Alan made a beeline for the drinks tray, holding up the bottle of Glenfiddich. She shook her head. Scotch wasn't a favourite of hers, but she almost changed her mind.

If Alan needed Dutch courage for what he had to say, maybe she needed some to hear him out.

"Make mine a red wine," she compromised, sitting in the armchair she usually occupied, her hands once again clutching each other to still their trembling.

After handing her the glass of merlot, Alan took a gulp from his own glass, then put it down on the table with a sharp crack, almost sloshing the contents over the rim, and began pacing.

Angie set hers down without taking so much as a sip, feeling it would choke her if she tried to drink.

At last, Alan turned to face her, leaning against the door jamb on the other side of the room.

"This isn't easy, Angie. Will you just listen before you say anything?" She nodded. "You thought, when I had difficulty agreeing to a date for our wedding, it was because I didn't really want to get married at all."

Alan took another steadying sip.

"I understand how my earlier behaviour made you jump to that conclusion, but it wasn't a case of not wanting to. I quite literally couldn't."

He looked away, shuffled a little, then straightened and came to the point.

"My fault again. I let you believe I was already divorced from Janice, but it's still with the lawyers. I don't know when it will be settled. After that night when I jumped the gun, asking you to marry me, I rang Jan to find out what the holdup was all about. Seems she couldn't be bothered with getting the divorce she'd asked for until she wanted to remarry, herself."

He paused for another sip, casting a surreptitious glance at Angie. He was relieved to see her sitting quietly, concentrating all her attention on his unfolding story.

"It should have been plain sailing, and all sorted by now. However, her lawyer went on holidays, then when he was back in the office, he dropped dead. Heart attack. He was a one-man-band, and his affairs were in shambles. Jan knew nothing of this until after I rang, then she started making enquiries. She got back to me Friday night. Before we bought the ring."

He paused again.

"Since then she's got another bloke onto it, but a lot of time was lost. He's hoping to have us sorted before the end of the year, but everything shuts down over Christmas and New Year, and he's warned us it could be as late as February, or even March. I've told my lawyer to do what he can to hurry it up, but you know what lawyers are."

Alan came to a halt, and when Angie continued to stare silently up at him, he abruptly sat down opposite her. She didn't look happy, but then, he'd known she wouldn't be.

Angie took her time processing the information. And containing the disappointment threatening to express itself in an angry outburst; although she couldn't hold it all in.

"For God's sake, Alan. You've claimed several times that you're an idiot. In my book, this proves it."

Now she was the one pacing the room.

Coming to a halt, she glared down at her lover, silently daring him to make some stupid excuse. When he showed sufficient common sense to keep his mouth shut, she flung herself down in her chair. Grabbing for her untouched wine, she tossed it down her throat with scant regard for its excellence.

"You hoped the lawyers would sort it all out, and I'd never need to know, didn't you?"

He nodded, relieved she wasn't taking it as badly as he'd feared.

"When it was obvious your tactics were upsetting me, why couldn't you have trusted me with the truth? Why wait so long? You must have known I'd understand."

The stunned expression on his face gave her the answer.

"You didn't trust me," she whispered, wounded to the core. "You wrote me off as too stupid to see the difference between something you'd done, and something out of your control."

She pushed herself awkwardly to her feet, her vision obscured by tears. *Damn him!* She swiped ineffectively at the flood.

"I want to go home," she sobbed.

"No, Darling. Please. Don't leave me. I couldn't bear it if you did."

Alan, following her towards the door, wrapped his arms around Angie, holding her against her shoulder.

"Don't cry," he murmured, rubbing her back as if comforting one of his daughters. He'd been afraid of her anger. Her pain, tearing at his heart, was so much worse.

At last Angie's sobs abated. Drawing her tear-sodden face from Alan's shoulder, she accepted the handkerchief he offered, turning away to dry her face and blow her nose. When she finished, he turned her gently to gaze earnestly into her eyes.

"The truth is, Angie, I was thinking of myself, not you. Not a mistake I'll be making again, that's for sure. I was afraid you'd wash your hands of me, bumbling idiot that I am. Far from thinking you stupid, you're just about the smartest person I know; with the possible exception of Edith Turner."

His lips quirked as he sought to lighten the atmosphere with his silly joke. To his relief, Angie giggled.

"You're right there, Darling. Eddie doesn't let anyone pull the wool over her eyes."

"Angelica," Alan knelt at her feet. "I love you, truly and forever. Will you marry me and put me out of my misery? Just as soon as I'm free," he added, when her raised brow reminded him of the state of play between them.

"I can't give you an exact day, but I promise, when I get the go-ahead, we'll be married as quickly as you like."

"Yes. Yes, to all of that." Angie tugged him to his feet and threw her arms around his neck. She felt light-headed, almost dizzy, without the leaden weight of suspicion dragging at her spirits. Peeking coyly from beneath her still-damp lashes, she suggested,

"Now we've settled the future, maybe you could use the present to show me how much you love me?" A suggestion Alan was only too happy to comply with.

~~~~~

Angie stretched, feeling content and very, very well used after the night, and early morning, of exemplary make-up sex.

She reached out to sift her fingers through Alan's dark, sweat-dampened curls. He claimed her hand, bringing it to his lips, and began kissing his way from finger to finger, ending with a last, moist kiss to the palm. About to leave that hand and begin on the other, he hesitated, looking at his fiancée sprawled at his side.

"Now that we've sorted out our problems, you can wear your ring, Ang. On the way into town, shall we take a detour via the farm to collect it?"

He couldn't wait to see his engagement ring on Angie's finger, the symbol of his successful courtship. A success all the sweeter for the setbacks they had suffered.

About to agree, Angie paused, wrinkling her forehead.

"Nooo," she said slowly. "Not yet, Darling. I really love our ring, and I do want to wear it, but it would be a public declaration, wouldn't it? Then we'd have to explain why we weren't making wedding plans, and everyone would be teasing us."

Alan opened his mouth, but she laid her fingers across it to silence him.

"Your mates would make you the butt of their jokes, and I'd hate that, Alan. I'd rather wait till we're ready to go ahead and set the date. If what you said is correct, hopefully it won't be too long."

Alan argued, but mindful of all he'd put Angie through, he conceded defeat when she remained adamant.

He just hoped they wouldn't be kept waiting for months.

16

"Let's get some takeaway and eat it in the park, over by the creek, Angie darlin'. I want to have a serious conversation, and if we stay here, everyone wandering by will want to stop and chat."

"Okay." Angie agreed willingly enough, although she wondered what was up. Alan had been acting slightly disgruntled for the last week or so, but she had put that down to the frustration caused by the loss of their cottage.

It belonged to Barbara, and she had finally acquired a long-term tenant who had wanted immediate occupancy. While neither of them begrudged Barbara her good fortune; at the same time, it did make finding a location for the private time which was so important to them both, rather awkward.

She was so looking forward to tomorrow, when she had arranged to swap her Friday night with Jodie.

Alan was taking her to Tamworth, and they wouldn't be back in The Crossing until she started work Saturday night.

"So, Alan. What was it you wanted to talk about?" Angie prompted. The picnic lunch had been consumed, and it was almost time for her to go on duty.

Alan had avoided getting serious, not wanting to introduce a discordant note; but damn it all, this was important to him. He'd agreed to every last thing Angie had asked of him, and now it was her turn.

"Angelica. Darling," he hesitated, then began again. "Angie, I know you don't agree with me on this, but it's really important to me. I've thought it over, and today I'm insisting ..."

Alan drew in a sharp breath, closing his eyes as if in pain. He knew as soon as he said the word, that it was a mistake, but there was no going back now. Best to plough on and hope she didn't notice.

"Angie, I want you to wear your engagement ring. I want everyone to know you're mine."

The words fired rapidly from his mouth, not allowing Angie time to get a word in.

"I know what you said, but I don't agree. We can simply tell anyone who asks that we haven't decided on a date yet."

How dare he 'insist'? Angie, fuming over Alan's unwise choice of words, barely heard the rest. When Alan held the ring box out, she automatically took it from him, opening it to look once more at the lovely ring they had chosen together.

"What do you say, Ang? Will you wear it for me?"

Looking up, Angie was repelled by his look of grim determination. She frowned. Why did he want to change things? They'd been getting along so well for the last few weeks, and they surely wouldn't have to wait much longer for the lawyers to get his divorce sorted.

She could wait.

She studied Alan's face, uncomfortably aware that they teetered on the brink of a fight. One she didn't want. Something had happened to stir Alan up like this. She asked, but he shook his head.

"I just want to see my ring on your finger," he stubbornly reiterated. Not waiting for her reply, he jumped to his feet.

"You're not going to do it, are you, Angie. It's all got to be your way. I ask one thing of you, and you won't even consider it. I've got to go. There's work I should be doing."

Her mouth open, Angie slowly rose to her feet, staring after Alan striding across the park to his ute. She still hadn't moved when he slammed the door shut and drove off in a flurry of gravel and dust, without a backward glance.

Shaking, she looked down at the ring box still clasped in her hand, her fingers cramping from their tight grip.

What had just happened?

Half an hour later, as she came down from her room to start work, she was still wondering. Her anger at being treated so rudely had flowed freely while she changed, but she'd had to reign it in and show a smiling face to the customers, even though the dregs still simmered deep inside. As the afternoon wore on, she found herself less angry and more concerned.

Her mind teemed with questions to which she didn't have time to find answers. Normally, she enjoyed her work. Tonight, she couldn't wait to finish up and escape to her room. Away from the brain-deadening thump, thump, thump of the jukebox being played so loudly she couldn't hear herself think.

She was on her dinner break when Alan phoned. Her relieved, "Alan, Darling, ..." was cut short.

"Are you wearing it?" His peremptory question took her aback.

"Well, ... Not just yet, Darling," she prevaricated. "I didn't want anyone ..." He didn't give her time to finish.

"Do you intend to?"

Annoyed at being cut off mid-sentence, she didn't try again to tell him she didn't want anyone telling his parents before they did. Instead, she snapped back,

"I'm thinking about it. We can discuss it tomorrow."

"Think hard, Angie," he said, hanging up on her. She immediately called him back, but he'd switched off his phone.

She gasped, clutching at the searing pain in her chest. They loved each other. Didn't they? She knew she loved Alan. She squeezed her eyes shut, breathing deeply until she had her emotions under control.

~~~~~

Sleep refused to come. Angie's mind circled round and round, getting nowhere.

Exhaustion finally overtook her, and she spent the remaining hours tossing and turning in restless sleep. It seemed she had barely closed her eyes when they sprang open again.

Desperately tired, but clear-headed, she knew she'd never get to sleep again, so she got up, even though it was still dark outside. Not even the birds were stirring.

Making a cup of tea, she curled up in her armchair by the window, cradling its warmth in her hands as she took stock of the clarity her subconscious had brought to her tumultuous thoughts of the night before.

Now she knew what she had been doing wrong.

With knowledge, the path forward was obvious, but in no way easy. Now her fear was that she had arrived at this state of mental clarity too late.

Urgency impelled her to shower and dress immediately. She had to get out to 'Morgan's Run'. Right now. If she waited for Alan to come to her, she would have lost forever this chance to set things right between them. Permanently. Cursing her lack of a vehicle, she cast about in her mind for a friend in town who wouldn't mind driving her to the farm before breakfast.

$$\sim\sim\sim\sim\sim$$

Alan, his heart heavy, was up early to get as much done as possible before going to meet Angie.

Although he wondered if there was any point now. Yesterday, he'd thrown down the gauntlet, and feared he'd lost the gamble. And the girl?

His Angie hadn't taken his challenge very well.

Losing his temper and refusing to take her call last night wouldn't have gone down well, either.

All he could do now was apologise. And grovel. And hope she'd forgive him again.

But damn-it-all, he still felt he'd been in the right, wanting to publicly declare their engagement. He was tired of hiding the truth of his love for Angie.

From the kennels down behind the sheds, he heard the noise of an approaching vehicle. Frowning, he turned to intercept the visitors, whoever they were, before they went banging on the front door, waking the rest of the family.

Worry over Angie making sleep hard to come by, was the reason he was up and about so bloody early. By the time he was in sight of the front of the house, all that remained of the unreasonably early visitation was a cloud of dust retreating down the track.

And one lonely, red-haired figure standing by the house gate, staring up at the front door.

"Angie!"

Alan called, waving to catch her eye. Unsure whether her presence signalled hope or disaster, he opted for hope, running to catch her up in his arms; holding on for dear life. When she flung her arms around his waist, grabbing handfuls of his shirt as if she intended to never let go, he breathed a sigh of relief, bending his head to claim the rosy lips raised to meet him half-way.

"Oh, Angie," he murmured. "I'm so sorry I ..."

"Shhh, Darling. You have nothing at all to be sorry for. I'm the one who's sorry. You were right to expect me to be completely open and honest about our engagement."

Angie cupped Alan's face between both hands, and he turned his head to place a kiss in her palm. Her left palm. He drew back, a puzzled look on his face.

"But … Angie, if you mean what you said, why are you still not …"

Again, Angie shushed him.

"I'm getting to that. Can we sit down and be comfortable, Alan? I've got quite a bit I need to say to you, then I promise I'll listen to everything you want to say."

Silently Alan led her to the nearest garden bench where they both sat, angled to watch each other closely. Eyes cast down, Angie twisted her fingers in her lap, sorting her thoughts into coherent order.

Half-afraid, despite their rapturous greeting, Alan contained his impatience.

"Before I came to Oxley Crossing," Angie began, low-voiced, eyes still downcast, "most of the men I was involved with, either family or romantically, were … disappointing. I was horribly betrayed more than once, and in self-defence, I grew suspicious of men and their promises. I developed a need to be in control all the time to protect myself from hurt. Since coming here, I've learned not all men are like those ones, but you were so awful at first, Alan, you ended up lumped in with the bad ones."

Nervously, she watched Alan, half afraid her words would arouse his quick temper.

Seeing no adverse signs, she took heart and continued.

"When you returned my love, I thought I had learned to trust you completely, but yesterday showed me I hadn't. Not completely. A tiny part of me was still expecting our love to end badly. It wasn't till I had time to think clearly, with no interruptions, that I came to see myself clearly. What I saw horrified me, Alan."

At this point, she looked up, lips trembling and her eyes tear-filled pools of darkest emerald. Alan took her hands in his, squeezing them reassuringly, waiting for her to finish.

"I do trust you, Alan. I really do. I'm certain of that now. I know you were let down too, growing bitter and disillusioned, but you've changed. Yesterday, when you asked me to demonstrate my trust, I failed you. Several times, you've proclaimed yourself an idiot, but Alan, I know it's really me who is the idiot. Can you ever forgive me?"

By now the tears were spilling over, running silently down Angie's cheeks.

Alan followed his instincts, scooping Angie onto his lap and hugging her to his heart.

"Course I forgive you, you silly idiot. We're a real pair, aren't we? Two idiots with nothing to choose between us. I understand what you said, my Darling. Does all that mean you're still willing to risk marrying me?"

Angie thumped his arm to make him loosen his grip. When she had space to move, she reached up to kiss him.

"Yes. I do still want to marry you, but it won't be a risk. Not for me, and not for you, either."

She started wriggling on his lap, struggling to get down.

"Let me up, Alan." Standing on the ground in front of him, she swung the small backpack she'd been wearing off her shoulders and began rummaging in the side pocket, emerging triumphant, a small, velvet covered jeweller's box which Alan remembered quite well, in her hand.

"Let's start again, shall we?" she asked, handing him the box.

$$\sim\sim\sim\sim\sim$$

Breakfast was a noisy celebration, with Andrew bringing out the bottle of champagne he'd stashed in the back of the fridge, just in case it might be needed. In all the to-do, the girls missed their school bus, and ended up helping their father with his chores so he could drive them to school before continuing to Tamworth with Angie.

Alone at last, Alan nonchalantly handed Angie an opened, registered letter.

"Present for you, Ang," he said, letting the engine idle till she had opened it. She drew out the official looking document, reading it carefully. Mouth open, she looked at Alan.

"Is this what I think it is?"

"Yep. My Decree Absolute. It arrived yesterday morning. I meant to share it with you then, but …" He shrugged. The less said about yesterday the better.

"We're having lunch with Mum's sister, Aunt Fiona."

Angie nodded. She had heard Barbara talk about her sister, and her heart lifted at what she thought was coming next.

"She's a marriage celebrant in her spare time," Alan said, shrugging diffidently "I thought it might be nice to have her officiate for us. You can work out the dates with her."

Angie's ear-splitting squeal of joy turned a few heads among the crowd of dispersing parents outside the school gate.

~~~~~

After a quick phone call to clear the date with Barbara, they settled on New Year's Eve; a few days past the mandatory one month's wait.

"I can't think of a better day to get married," Angie whispered in Alan's ear.

"A new year, and a new life together."

THE END

I hope that you enjoyed 'Marrying Alan Morgan'.

Turn the page for a preview of the next book in the 'Love in Oxley Crossing' Series – 'Saving Jonathon Armitage'.

Here is Your Preview of
Saving Jonathon Armitage

Love in Oxley Crossing – Book 2

LENA WEST

1

"Oh, very nice." Megan Patterson shifted for a clearer view of the service station apron.

"What? What's very nice? C'mon Megs, give."

"Sorry Geni. Momentarily distracted. I was admiring a very nice, late model Harley that pulled in for fuel just now. Black with chrome trim. Never mind, go on with what you were saying."

Megan shifted the phone to her other ear, eyes still glued to the motorbike that had caught her eye.

"Never mind the Harley, Megs. What's the Harley's rider like? He's got to be more interesting than my rant about my soon-to-be ex. Is he a spunk, or a hog?"

"A spunk, far as I can see."

Megan laughed as she always did when Geni voiced her nonsensical interest in some man. Any man.

"Tell me more. You know Megs, this is half your trouble, you know," Geni Sullivan's voice took on a censorious tone.

"If, just occasionally, you noticed the man rather than the machine, you might have landed yourself one by now and be happy as a pig in mud with half a dozen kids and an adoring husband. So, let's start practising. Right now. Go on, take a good look at this bloke on the Harley and tell me what you see."

Megan laughed again, then decided to play along with her friend. After all, Geni still lived in Sydney. Too far away to push her into any more blind dates or difficult foursomes in her crusade to 'find Megan a man'.

In Megan's opinion, Geni was a prime example of the problems you incurred if you chose badly, ending up with someone who fell way short of being Mr Absolutely Perfect. With the example of her parents' happy, loving marriage as her benchmark, she'd long ago decided she'd rather wait till she was sure.

Only she hadn't really expected the wait to be so long.

Just lately she'd seriously begun to question whether she'd set her expectations unreasonably high. Thinking that maybe she ought to settle for Mr Pretty Good.

Shaking herself out of her moment of introspection she applied herself to Geni's exercise.

"Let's see." The subject of the exercise was swinging a long, well-proportioned leg over the bike propped onto its stand beside the pump. Megan's eyes opened a little wider, studying the man now with a coolly critical, though admiring eye. And she found plenty to admire.

"Tall, black leathers, snug fitting," she began reciting, then continued. "Oh good, no club insignia. Lean, slim-hipped. A derrière my palms itch to fondle."

She grinned, knowing Geni would appreciate the titillating extra.

"Keep going, you're doing fine."

"Don't be so impatient Geni. Ah, the helmet's off."

The man shook out a sweat-damp, dark wavy mane that brushed his shoulders, so Megan added that to her description.

"Can't see his face yet. Oh, he's taking off his jacket, Geni. White T-shirt, sweat stained. Must be hot under the helmet and full leathers, even though the weather's still a bit cool. Broad shoulders, good muscle definition. Lean, work-hardened muscles, you know, not pumped up from working out in the gym."

Megan ran out of steam at that point. Until the man turned his face towards her, she had nothing to add. Nothing she cared to tell Geni, anyway. No way was she going to tell her friend about the butterflies stirring in her stomach.

No way.

If she did, she'd never hear the end of it. Just the same, she let her eyes rove over the attractive masculine figure outside the office window, this time solely for her own pleasure.

Hanging up the nozzle, the rider turned to walk into the office; and the butterflies fluttered their wings.

"Early thirties I'd guess. Good-looking," she added to the tally then finished up in a hurry.

"Gotta go Geni. He's coming in. Bye."

Snapping the phone off before her friend had time to say another word, she slipped it into the pocket of her tattered gardening jeans.

Lively blue eyes tracked the Harley's rider through the door. A smile still lingering on her face from the nonsense with Geni, Megan surreptitiously studied the high cheeked-boned, tanned face; mouth drying and smile fading as the butterflies beat their wings more energetically.

Alarmed at her unexpected physical reaction, Megan gulped, struggling to quell a sudden attack of nerves when, totally shocked, she identified her unfamiliar feelings as pure lust.

Ignoring her, he crossed straight to the fridge, helping himself to a carton of chocolate milk; her favourite too. Was that a good sign or not?

'Sign of what, for God's sake?'

Half-heartedly, she tried to divert her thoughts only to fail in the next instant.

Impatiently tearing the carton open he gulped the milk down straight from the carton. A tendril of sensual delight curled upward through Megan's body and her fingers longed to reach out and sweep those untidy locks back from the wide forehead as her eyes followed the swallowing movement of the Adam's apple bobbing in his throat.

Embarrassed by her unwonted voyeurism, Megan strove to banish her alarming reactions to this chance-encountered stranger.

'It's Geni's fault,' she grumbled to herself, *'making me way too aware of his attractions.'* It wasn't her normal practice to ogle strangers as if she'd never seen a good-looking man before.

'Still,' an inner voice that sounded a lot like Geni argued, *'it's a free world. A girl can always look, can't she?'* Surely there was no harm in that. Even so, Megan had the uncomfortable presentiment she was straying onto dangerous ground, and hurriedly dropped her eyes. Just in time.

The rider turned face-on, for the first time giving Megan an unobstructed view of shuttered, steely grey eyes and a tight, keep-your-distance expression.

She shivered, the butterflies folding their wings abruptly when she encountered chilly indifference in the look turned on her by the man she'd been guiltily fantasising over.

Megan had little personal vanity, her self-image being of wholesome ordinariness instead of the alluring siren she'd once dreamed of becoming. During her early years she had been consistently passed over as girlfriend material by the male of the species.

As a child she had been a tomboy, a welcome extra to make up the cricket or football team; later a knowledgeable admirer of their cars, the confidante to whom they poured out their troubles. Always their buddy, but never any man's love.

Apparently, whatever it was that attracted men in *that* way was in short supply in herself; a fact she'd long been reconciled to. Confidant of one day finding her own particular mate, and unwilling to settle for second best, Megan had refused to let it trouble her, enjoying herself without becoming too closely involved with the men she'd met in the city.

Attractive, entertaining men some of them, but none who affected her deeply.

No man had ever touched her guarded heart.

Instinct warned her that this man was intangibly different.

This man aroused unfamiliar longings within her. Disturbing longings to be more than she knew herself to be. More beautiful. More vivacious. *'More sexy,'* whispered that treacherous inner voice. More everything.

With a disparaging downwards glance at her appalling gardening clothes a sigh issued silently through lips that momentarily assumed an unaccustomed droop.

Stranger though he was, this man's coldness for some inexplicable reason, had the power to hurt her.

'The sooner he's on his bike and out of here again, the better,' she thought crossly, mentally shaking off her pain as she accepted his money.

Defiantly meeting his eyes with a stare aloof enough to match his own, Megan accidentally brushed his fingers as she handed over his change. A tiny, but very definite, electric charge almost had her dropping the coins. Nothing like *that* had ever happened to her before! Startled by the unexpected tingle, she stifled a gasp and had to work at retaining her equilibrium.

Instead of taking himself off immediately, the oh-so-annoying man hovered in front of Megan, as if trying to make up his mind about something.

"Anything else I can help you with?" she asked, professionally polite, still matching him cool stare for cool stare while willing him on his way.

Abruptly making his mind up, he nodded towards the sign in the window.

**MECHANIC WANTED
APPLY WITHIN**

"That job. Is it still available?" His low baritone, heard for the first time, matched his cold expression.

Megan's heart sank.

The Lord knew, she desperately needed to find a mechanic, and soon, or her father's garage would be forced to close. His customers were loyal, but they couldn't be expected to wait forever. Work was piling up and soon his customers would be turning elsewhere.

Only couldn't her first applicant, make that only applicant, have been someone who didn't unsettle her as this man did?

"Yes, the job's still available," she answered reluctantly. "Are you applying for it?"

Megan had to work even harder now to keep her own voice and eyes cool and non-committal.

He nodded, eyes sliding past Megan to look out the window. Dismissing her. As if making up his mind, he swung to face her again, his gaze now sharply focused.

"Who do I talk to?"

So he was serious. Megan bit her lip, thinking quickly. Her need for a mechanic outweighed her personal wariness; and, she reminded herself, beggars couldn't afford to be choosers. Since she'd received no other expressions of interest, she ought to be jumping for joy instead of wanting to brush him off.

"You talk to me," she stated crisply, decision made. "I take it you have all the necessary paperwork. Trade qualifications, references, etcetera?"

All business now, Megan looked him in the eye, informing him in no uncertain manner that she was in charge.

"In my saddlebags." He hesitated, and Megan cut in, eager now not to let opportunity slip through her fingers.

"Go and get them then, why don't you. You're here anyway and since it's a slow morning I can fit in an interview right away, if you like."

Shrugging, he went outside and moved his bike away from the pumps before digging in the saddlebag for his document folder.

God knew, he needed a job, but did it have to be out here in the middle of nowhere? He'd seen an ad in the 'Tamworth Times' at breakfast, and on impulse had decided to try for it. Only Oxley Crossing was way out in the sticks, and he was a city boy. What the bloody hell was he doing out here?

He'd almost turned back, after miles of nothing but bush, dusty sheep and widely scattered farmhouses; except that his stubborn streak had kicked in, insisting he follow through on what he'd started.

'Looks like I'm about to rejoin the ranks of the employed,' he thought sourly. He wouldn't be staying long though, just until he had a few dollars in his kitty again; then they wouldn't see him for dust.

The few shops he'd noticed on his slow burbling progression down the main street had represented all the basic necessities, and a handful of extras, but absolutely nothing in the way of entertainment except for the pub. Not his kind of town, that's for sure.

Offering coffee, or another cold drink if he preferred, Megan led the way to one of the tables across the room from the cash register. Immediately setting a friendly, impersonal tone for the interview, she introduced herself, extending her hand to him as she did so.

"Megan Patterson. My father owns this service station and garage. Usually he runs it himself, but he's laid up for a month or two and we need a stand-in mechanic."

There it was again! That electric tingle when their hands touched. Frowning briefly, he glanced at his hand, then shook it slightly and wiped it across his shirt as he took his seat.

So, he felt it too. Megan wondered fleetingly what caused it. *'Probably just static electricity,'* she answered herself, then concentrated her mind on the interview.

"Jon Armitage," the biker offered in response to Megan's introduction. "So you're only looking for someone on a temporary basis. How long for?"

"It depends on the doctors, really, but I expect it will be a minimum of two to three months." *'Please don't let him be put off by the lack of permanency,'* Megan prayed silently.

The ads in the papers had been running for over a week already, producing no more interest than the sign in the window. Until today. Few people were interested in working in a little country place like Oxley Crossing; even fewer when the job was temporary.

"Two or three months should be okay," Jon agreed after taking a moment to consider." I take it it's a one-man operation? No apprentices or assistants?"

"That's right. Just Dad, since he took over from my grandfather twenty years ago. You wouldn't have to worry about the pumps at all, we have other people to handle that; just the mechanical side. If you're interested, let me see your papers. If they're satisfactory, we can talk business."

As Megan browsed carefully through his file, stopping to clarify a point here and there, Jonathon Armitage went up a notch or two in her estimation. It required an effort not to let him see how impressed she was.

"Good qualifications," Megan conceded coolly. "The references look good too, but you do realise I'll have to verify them, don't you?" she challenged, looking him straight in the eye.

"Of course. No problem." He shrugged, totally unconcerned.

'*He's very confident they'll check out well,*' Megan observed. She had begun to see Jonathon Armitage in a new light; as a potential asset for the business.

And for herself? Shocked, she shied away from answering that question, wondering where it had sprung from. '*Damn Genie and her nonsense.*'

"How long do you expect that to take you?"

Jonathon Armitage's question pulling her attention back from disturbing personal questions to the business at hand, Megan calculated swiftly.

"If I can reach your referees immediately, no more than an hour or so. I'll get on the phone right away. In the meantime, why don't you take a look around the town. Have some lunch. By then I should be able to give you an answer."

Megan gave him a cool, professional smile and waved him towards the door; this time carefully avoiding his hand. Most likely it was only static electricity she felt when they touched; but then again, maybe it wasn't.

Nodding his agreement, Jon walked off, passing an older man just entering; one who wore a petroleum company logo on his uniform jacket.

Lean and balding with a droopy moustache, he frowned forbiddingly at the darkly handsome young man in black leathers and T-shirt.

"Who was that young fella Meggie? It's not like you to sit around with strangers who blow into town." Half inquisitive and half protective, he let his concern for Megan show, defusing her flash of irritation at his implied criticism.

Jack O'Hara had been best man at her parents' wedding; had known her all her life, always treating her like one of his own daughters. Knowing his nosiness was kindly meant, Megan welcomed him with a warm smile.

"That young fella, Jack," she informed him smugly, "is our new mechanic. As long as his references are as good as they look. His trade qualifications are excellent. Now that you're back, I'll head over to my own office. Send him across when he comes back, will you please, Jack?"

Continued…….

Get

"Saving Jonathon Armitage"

as soon as it's released – go to

www.lenawestauthor.com

and make sure that you are signed up for news and release notices!

About the Author

Born in tropical North Queensland, Lena loves living close to the sea, although she moved frequently during her early years, living everywhere from large cities to isolated farms. Her most recent home has a deck overlooking the ocean, which is her favourite room in the house, for reading, writing, art, craft or even birdwatching, when the local birds come to visit.

After working as a primary school teacher in both her native Queensland, and later in New South Wales where she met her own romantic hero, she took a very early retirement to travel Australia with him, in a motorhome. This idyllic lifestyle lasted several years, during which time she indulged in the creation of story plots and their settings, culminating in her taking steps to fulfil her lifelong ambition to write.

Storytelling came naturally - she had been making up stories for her own entertainment all her life, but it wasn't until she began traveling that she had time to write down some of her favourites. Now published, *Marrying Alan Morgan*, is the first in a series of rural romances set in the fictional town of Oxley Crossing. It is followed by the soon to be released second in the series, *Saving Jonathon Armitage,* with several more in the series planned. She also writes standalone contemporary romances and Australian historical romances.

She has an addiction to happily-ever-afters, in both her reading and her own stories, so the romance genre was a natural fit, and the variety of places she has lived have all added to the settings in which she brings love to life.

You can find Lena on Facebook at:

https://www.facebook.com/LenaWestAuthor/

or sign up for her newsletter at :

www.lenawestauthor.com

Other Books by Lena West

Standalone Contemporary Romances

Loving Fenella (Coming soon)

Bronwyn's Family (Coming soon)

Contemporary Series

The Wylde Flower Series (Coming soon)

Historical Romances

Unto Death (Coming soon)

Emily's Baby (Coming soon)

Home is the Heart (Coming soon)

Blue Streak (Coming soon)

Love and War (Coming soon)

Books in the
Love in Oxley Crossing Series

Marrying Alan Morgan

Saving Jonathon Armitage (Coming soon)

Finding Mr Wright (Coming soon)

Electing Robert Whitman (Coming soon)

Redeeming Josh Marten (Coming soon)

(and more to follow!)

Connect with Lena!

Be the first to know about it when Lena's next book is released!

Sign up to Lena's newsletter at

www.lenawestauthor.com